Acts of Consequence

Best Wishes to Margaret.
Alva.

Acts of Consequence

Alva de Chiro

First published in Great Britain in 2014 by

Bannister Publications Ltd
118 Saltergate
Chesterfield
Derbyshire S40 1NG

Typeset in Palatino Linotype by Escritor Design,
Chesterfield, Derbyshire

Printed and bound in Great Britain by
SRP Ltd, Exeter, Devon

I would like to thank the following people for their help in this writing venture.
Carlo for his technical assistance.
Heather and Freda for their on-going encouragement and Pam for her patience and generous help in proof-reading my stories.

Contents

Coffee, Cupcakes and Candour   1

The Best Things in Life Are Free   7

Catherine, a Queen Betrayed   13

Tasty Persuasions   17

Darkness and Light   21

How the Mighty Have Fallen   27

Unexpected Joy   33

Paints a Thousand Words   37

It Could Have Been Worse   41

A Watery Grave   45

An English Girl Abroad....
Introducing Mamma   51

Behind the Grease Paint   55

The Chandelier's Story   61

Losing Face   67

Jack and Jill   71

The Letter   77

Sun.... Sand.... and Sacrifice   85

The Golden Wedding Anniversary   89

Coffee, Cupcakes and Candour

'If only you were more adventurous Thelma,' complains Betty, as we sip our chocolate-dusted coffees. We meet every Thursday in The Azure Coffee House, blue and silver walls surround us, and tempting aromas filter appetisingly into every corner and out into the street.

Betty is scooping and digesting the escapees, crumbs that have landed on her ample chest. Raised eyebrows signal that she is awaiting a response.

'In.... what.... way ?' I manage to stutter.

'Oh, in every way,' she replies dismissively, 'your dress sense for one. Well let's face it Thelma, you always dress in beige and pearls, very dowdy. Your hobbies! she snorts with uncontrollable laughter, more crumbs parachute onto the table. 'Don't tell me that knit and natter is electrifying?'

I begin to form my answer, but Betty's there first, she anticipates my reply and butts in with, 'Please don't say that they are lovely people.'

Totally unaware of my discomfort, she continues, 'I'll take you shopping. I'll be your fashion advisor.'

A quiet and yet penetrating voice invades my thoughts, churns my innards. "Remember to be a good girl for mummy or mummy won't be able to give you a cuddle when you go to bed. Be polite and always say, yes thank you."

'Thank you Betty, that will be lovely,' as my mouth utters those words.... an image of Betty as a fierce headmistress

1

brandishing a bendy cane, pops into my mind. I'm unsure if it's a silent retaliation, a reaction to being unable to say no. I will have to resign myself to being a people pleaser.

I emerge from Debenham's with a short orange skirt that emphasises my fat dimpled knees and a lime-green jacket that sits, oh so snugly, on my derrière! Within days a Save the Children collection bag leans against my gate post. I hope the contents are enjoyed by someone.

It's Thursday. I'm in the coffee-house, just about to take a sip of latte when an explosive shower of coffee droplets hit the glass table like thundery rain on a pavement. It is uncontrollable. Betty just has time to rescue her treacle flapjack from the liquid attack. I have just received the news that Betty has signed us up for a parachute jump!

'A... a... parachute jump?' They're the only words I can manage to utter.

My silence encourages Betty to keep talking and munching, she assures me it is for a good cause, the R.N.L.I. A picture of her in a Casino, flashes into my mind. Whilst all is hushed, she, gambler extraordinaire brandishes on high the trump card, adorned with a life boat being tossed on rough seas. She throws it down onto the table. Invincible Betty!

I am about to jump, skidding fast below me are the hills and dales of Derbyshire. I am strapped into my parachute, and am gazing down and down and down. Betty developed sciatica yesterday and says she is in acute pain. I'm suffering from acute fear. However there is a slight plus I am clasped tightly to a parachute professional. We jump. I land safely. Grassy fields ready and welcoming for my roly-poly landing. I begin to breathe again.

Coffee and cup cakes seem to energise Betty. Today, I am informed that I am enrolled at the local W.E.A. Egyptology classes. Betty says, 'It's time to do something cultural.'

'I do agree,' I reply, whilst thinking, I've never been really interested in history, but something stronger than me insists that I say, 'yes thank you'. But I am relieved that I'm not signed up to scale the wall of death or do a bungee jump.

Betty has left the Egyptology class she says, 'It's boring'. I continue. I'm getting absorbed in the subject and am eager to learn more about these people who lived so long ago, but whose legacy remains today. Secretly I am also attending self assertive classes, and I seem to be flourishing at those too. Life's taken on a new slant.

I went on a shopping spree on my own and emerged with an aqua trouser suit, a cream top and a necklace with turquoise gob-stopper beads. The kind that makes a statement. Sahbi, our Egyptology teacher always seems to compliment me on my appearance.

I wear my new outfit the next time I meet Betty. She scans me up and down, but makes no comment, that means I'm looking good. I order the usual latte and prepare myself to listen. After a few bites of cup-cake, Betty's future programme for me unfolds.

'We need a change, trailing round town every day, looking in the same shops is boring.' A statement not to be challenged.

'What did you have in mind?' I inquire, with not a hint of trepidation. I've been learning that the most polite people are permitted to say no.

'A week in Spain will fit the bill. We can walk on the promenade. Stop and have a coffee. Go on a few trips and have a game of Bingo at night. I was thinking of booking on the sixteenth of this month.'

Sipping my coffee I'm pondering how I'm going to tell Betty that the holiday in Spain is not going to materialise for me. The fact that I am not responding immediately, with my usual words of, "that will be lovely," seems to be unnerving her. Glinting eyes and raised eyebrows are signs of impatience and attack.

'Come on Thelma, what are you thinking about? Don't know what's got into you these days always appearing in a new outfit, blonde streaks and painted nails.'

So she has noticed but has been too mean spirited to say so.

Placing my cup down carefully, I look straight at her and say, 'Sorry Betty, I won't be able to go.'

Crumbs fly everywhere. Coffee overflows into the saucer and it seems that I must have developed Medusa like powers for Betty's face is frozen, in a kind of caricature. I'm wondering if her mouth will ever close again and her eye brows resume their natural position. The picture that pops into my mind is one of those comic postcards of an overblown wife in a flowered dress beating her undersized, erring husband. Unfortunately for Betty, but fortunate for me, she hasn't got an umbrella with her today.

'Not able to go,' she finally utters. 'Why ever not?'

'I'll be away. Sahbi, you remember the lecturer on Egyptology has arranged for a small group of us to go to Egypt, with him as our guide.'

That statement does not help Betty regain her equilibrium.

'I've never heard anything like it in my life you must be mad. You'll undoubtedly come back with typhoid, cholera or even rabies, because there'll be plenty of mad dogs there,' she finishes triumphantly.

'I've had a few jabs and I don't think we'll be slumming it, in a five star hotel.' Self assertive classes are definitely working.

Now Betty's turned into the Medusa. With a glance that could turn anyone to stone, she gulps down her chocolate brownie and coffee, gathers up her straw shopping bag and sweeps out. I remain. Sipping my latte and watching the

4

shoppers in their varied shapes and attires hurry past. My mind is filled with pictures of Egypt.

We are walking through the streets of Cairo, loud and unwieldy. Haphazard motorists, showing no concern for the Highway Code! As I pick my way carefully along uneven pavements, the familiar rich smell of coffee wafts into my nostrils, mingling with an aromatic incense-like scent.

'What is that smell?' I ask.

'It's the smell of a tobacco that has been cured in molasses. It is being smoked in a shisha or a water-pipe, perhaps better known to you as a Hubbly Bubbly,' Sahbi replies, as he guides us along towards the museum.

'The treasures of the tomb of the young Pharaoh were discovered in 1922 and was probably the greatest archaeological find ever made,' he explains. 'I imagine you can appreciate the skill of the goldsmiths at this time and note how the gold is inlaid with lapis lazuli, quartz, turquoise and coloured glass.'

I feel overpowered by its splendour, and its testament to an age of superb craftsmen, who lived thousands of years ago.

'Notice the wooden throne, inlaid with minute pieces of ivory, ebony, precious stones and glass,' continues Sahbi. Details that could be easily overlooked without an enthusiastic guide.

We visit the Valley of the Kings, where Pharaohs were buried 3,000 years ago, and go down the many steps leading to the burial chamber. The walls that enclose us are covered by hundreds of hieroglyphics. Sahbi points out the scarab beetle.

'The scarab for the Egyptians then and today is a symbol of hope and restoration of life.' I spot scarabs everywhere on paintings, in stone and on jewellery.

After a week my Egyptian experience comes to an end. I want to see more. I've been enthralled and in awe of the artistry and beliefs of the ancient Egyptians.

'I'm really sorry it's over,' I confide to Sahbi.

'We can come again, one visit is never enough to see all the wonders that Egypt has to offer. By the way, a little gift for you.'

We are exploring the noisy bazaar, seething with veiled women, and assailed on all sides by shouts of, 'Marks and Spencer's quality for Primark prices.' The market sellers seem well informed about our shops.

I open the little box and there nestling on maroon velvet is a silvery scarab beetle with a turquoise body.

'Thank you,' I pause, as pictures run through my head. 'You couldn't have chosen a better present for me.' And in that moment I realise that I'm not just reciting those words to feel secure and win affection, but that I really mean them.

A few weeks later, I'm passing the Azure and decide to pop in for a latte. I sit in my favourite spot near the window, but keep checking my lapel where my scarab brooch glistens in the sunlight.

A voice penetrates my visions of lotus flowers and sunsets on the Nile. Betty is here. Her words are familiar, they conjure up a myriad of thoughts. Perhaps I should thank her for my transformation.

Yes, I'm not mistaken, she is saying to her unfortunate companion, "If only you were more adventurous!"

The Best Things in Life Are Free

'This is the house for me,' trilled Julia, as she danced from room to room, pausing now and again, to stroke the black granite tops in the kitchen. Admire the mulberry and grey decor of the entrance hall, and pose before its huge oval mirror, where she pouted, copying the expressions of celebrities in Hello Magazine.

'Remember, there's only the two of us,' said Tom, trying to quell the waves of nausea that were bubbling around inside him.

'Your two kids come every fortnight, they'll be able to have a room each, and perhaps we'll have more peace.'

'Ace card Julia' he muttered.

'I've decided, we're moving,' she proclaimed.

'We'll never afford to eat if we move here,' said Tom, as he climbed the oak steps, following Julia as she glided towards the master bedroom, as if she was the lady of the manor. And as he had anticipated, the silence was soon broken by shrieks of delight.

'Tom, even you won't be able to resist this.' She pulled him into the large room, fitted with built in wardrobes and a triple mirrored dressing table. 'Isn't this luxury with a capital L?'

Tom caught sight of himself in the mirror and thought that he looked old and ill. Where had it all gone wrong? He'd married Julia too soon after his divorce. He hadn't really known her. He had felt so lonely, when his boys had gone with their mother. But to his cost he had learned very quickly that Julia would get a first prize for sulking, and could keep up the non speaking game for days. He knew that if he refused to put down a deposit, his life would be hell.

'It's that all right,' he agreed, 'but we could not afford to live here unless you worked and we had two lots of wages coming in.'

'I can get a job, no prob. If I can live here, I'll be the happiest woman in the world. Shaz and Tracey, my up market friends will turn green, I can't wait to see their faces.'

She gave Tom a passionate kiss and moulded her body into his, whispering, 'I will show you a good time....'

A month later, they had moved. They were the owners of a stone built house of character. It seemed that all was well with the world and to Tom's surprise, Julia had taken on a new persona, that of the perfect housewife. Tom was kissed and sent off to work with tasty sandwiches and fruit, and returned home to a dust-free house, gleaming work tops and savoury aromas heralding roast chicken or lamb chops, or some other meaty delight from Delia's cook book. They dined formally, with a tall candelabra posed in the centre of the table. He did think it was over the top, but was so glad that Julia wasn't insisting that he wore a tuxedo. She seemed to be taking on the domestic role, like a duck to water. Perhaps he had misjudged her. But he did begin to worry as to when she might consider going to work.

One evening when they had arrived at the cheese-board course, Julia said,' I'm having Tracey and Shaz round tomorrow. I keep picturing their faces. They'll be jealous all right.' She spread some Brie onto the cracker and continued with her monologue. 'I can read you like a book. You're wondering if and when I'm going to get a job.'

Swallowing the Mexican spicy cheese quickly, Tom stuttered, 'To be truthful I was wondering.... but realise you've been busy with the unpacking and....'

8

Tom's speech was cut short.

'Meet the new receptionist of the Sandy Hills golf club. Had an interview today, computer skills sufficient, telephone manner, second to none. I start next Monday.'

'Congratulations!'

'I was getting so bored with playing the little housewife.'

Ignoring the fact that she was getting bored he decided to be totally positive.

'That's great, because we're running up a few bills.' Better understate it, he thought.

A routine began. Tom left at 8.30, having had cornflakes and packed his sandwiches. Julia got up as he was leaving, and when showered, perfumed, and dressed as if she was about to negotiate a banking deal in the city, left for Sandy Hills.

She was never there when Tom arrived home at 6pm. The silence was only broken by a ping, as the microwave plate completed its circling and the cottage pie or lasagne could be removed. He couldn't be bothered to cook for himself. He then settled down to watch the One Show and waited. And waited. His ears alert to every sound. Rustling leaves. Pattering rain drops. Sometimes Tom was so agitated that he would go into the garden, straining his ears for the sound of her car, inhaling the night air, until he gave up and wearily climbed the stairs to sleep in the guest room, although he thought wryly, they never had any guests. She'd explained with her she who must be obeyed voice, and with the last consonant of every word enunciated like a headmistress addressing a miscreant, that she didn't like to be disturbed in a morning, and preferred her own en-suite.

During his many sleepless nights Tom battled with his situation, he concluded that he was glad that it wasn't rows and sulks, but more like living apart together. He always hoped that tomorrow would be a better day, and yet a feeling of foreboding always overwhelmed him. He despised himself for acting like a wimp and yet his energies were nil. Sometimes he lay in bed waiting to hear the door click. She was keeping very late hours. He often sensed that she was crawling up the stairs. Too many glasses of Merlot or Prosecco, or tequilas, or mojitos, or any other alcoholic beverage.

Once he'd questioned the lateness. 'You're at that golf club most of the day.... and night.'

Julia had turned, anger exuding from every pore, and with eyes like slivers of black diamonds, hissed through bulbous lips, perhaps had Botox, thought Tom.

'You wanted me to get a job, I got one. But you're still not satisfied. Now I've got to clock in. Anyway all you do is watch the telly and fall asleep. I'm not a geriatric yet, I'm enjoying life. Having a good time. Get my drift? And don't forget I put up with your kids every fortnight.' The threat was always there, he often pondered why he didn't stand up to her, he just didn't like constant confrontation.

Tom knew the debts were piling up. He'd taken out a loan and the interest on that was phenomenal and he'd received a few warnings that the house would be re-possessed if some effort wasn't made to pay up. He'd discovered that whisky did help him to sleep and blot out terrifying scenarios, of bailiffs, removal men, court rooms and sleeping rough. Every minute of his working day in the car showrooms, when he was supposed to look dapper and smiling, was spent thinking, thinking of how he would tell Julia.

Tom sensed that his boss, Mr. Robinson had noticed the change in his appearance and his lack of success on the sales floor. But he also knew that Mr. Robinson was not a hasty man and was probably thinking that his once leading salesman was not well, or just going through a bad patch.

'Whatever's the matter? What are you doing in this shop door way? You're soaked and you're drunk', said Mr. Robinson as he helped Tom to his feet and led him to his car.

'You're coming home with me, and tomorrow morning we'll talk.' Tom wanted to lean on someone, he had reached rock bottom.

The following morning, as he and Mr. Robinson were having breakfast, Tom apologised again and again. Tom's words tumbled out, 'I've got into a lot of debt, we're going to lose the house. Julia will hate me and I might not be able to see my boys.'

'I can understand you trying to escape from your problems,' said Mr. Robinson in an understanding tone, 'but there is no escape and certainly getting drunk is not a solution. Now eat your breakfast. Take the rest of the week off. Go home smarten yourself up. Tell Julia, the whole story because she's probably as worried as you.'

Tom knew for certain that Julia was not worried at all. In fact when they happened to meet each other in the house, she looked as if she'd just returned from a tropical island. She was glowing, her skin had mahogany tones. She only needed a grass skirt to complete the picture. He blotted out the image and concentrated again on what Mr. Robinson was saying, 'And on the positive side you've still got your job'.

'Thank you, I'll do just as you suggest,' but whilst Tom was uttering these words, his fear of Julia's reaction was so great, that she kept appearing to him in high definition, striding towards him, like a warrior, with sucker-fish lips.

Tom knew that he had been saved. He'd been given a second chance. Mr. Robinson had given him courage. As he drove home, he realised that his boys, his Sam and James, were the most important people in his life, and with that thought in his mind he entered the house. It was silent. He glanced into the kitchen, not even a coffee cup on the work-top. He crept up the stairs and listened at her bedroom door. Silence. The kind that tells you that no one is in that room. He returned to the kitchen and there it was stuck to the silver door of the fridge.

What a loser. What did I ever see in you? I've met a real man, and I'm off to the Seychelles tomorrow, where he's got an apartment and lots of money. He's got a villa in Seville as well, so Tom, it's hasta la vista, adios, arrivederci and all the rest. Hope you can sort your bills out. Be thinking of you as I'm sipping Tequilas.   Julia.

Tom read it again and absorbed the words. He felt relieved, a huge weight had been lifted from his shoulders. He was glad she'd gone to sunny shores. She could get as wrinkled and brown as a walnut, and have more of her anatomy Botoxed to match the sea-life look she seemed to be gravitating towards.

He was now able to devote his full attention to his finances, or lack of them. At least he could move to a little terraced house that Mr. Robinson owned. He would have to work some evenings as well, perhaps in a restaurant or a pub. But he would be able to see his boys. He pictured all three of them in the park, having a game of football, or laughing at a video together. You didn't need stone-built houses, granite worktops, or candelabras to make you happy.

He took one last look around the house, and caught his reflection in the hall mirror. He remembered how haggard he'd looked when he'd glanced at himself last time, and yes he was thinner, but his head was not throbbing and his heart thumping, and he was not filled with apprehension. Surprisingly he felt liberated. You've learned a lot in a short time, he told himself. He had no doubt that there were still a lot of rocky hills to climb, and dark tunnels to go through. But like a mountaineer at the base of Everest, he was ready to climb to the summit and meet his tomorrow.

Catherine, a Queen Betrayed

'Madam, it has been discovered that your marriage must be annulled, it is stated in the Holy Bible that a man cannot marry his brother's wife.'

I was chilled by Wolsey's pronouncement. My thoughts raced. What was going to happen to me? What was going to happen to my daughter Mary? Were they going to send me away? Would I be spending the rest of my days in the Tower? Had I been summoned like a common prisoner to hear my sentence?

Coldness gripped me making my hands shake. I fingered the intricate swirls on my crucifix and prayed for strength and courage. I despised, Wolsey, I loathed him, this man who had been my teacher and most Catholic friend, now was a traitor and enemy .During these moments of calm I determined that I would not converse with him. Only with my husband. I turned my back and looked towards Henry, whose face was set as if in grey stone.

'My King, my husband of twenty-four years. Have I not served you well? Fulfilled my wifely duties? Acted as your ambassador? Supported you in every venture? Been faithful to you every day, every moment? My only failing, to provide you with a son and male heir, but with a healthy daughter....'

'And there we have it Madam,' interrupted Henry, and almost as an afterthought, 'there is also the fact that it is stated in the Holy Book that we should never have married.'

I knew in that moment, in a split second of clarity, that plotting and planning had won, the flag of treachery was triumphant over loyalty and love. I was defeated. Henry was determined to marry the Boleyn woman for whatever trumped up reason, but Wolsey's suggestion that I should go away quietly and spend the rest of my days in a convent, was not going to happen. I sensed that Henry still had some respect for me and was not going to condemn me to the Tower or to lose my head. No, he wanted me to disappear. Dissolve into nothingness, without a fuss. This disappearing act I am not going to do. His steely expression, somehow had strengthened me and gave me the resolve to fight back, even though I realised that the ultimate victory would be his. He would marry Anne Boleyn.

I hurried along the long corridors desperate to get back to my own room. To cry. To pray. To ask God and all the saints to support me at this darkest of times. I knelt by my bed and prayed. Prayed as I have never done before, asking God and the Virgin Mary to give me strength to survive these terrible feelings that were whirling inside me, pulsing in my stomach, thudding in my heart and beating in my head. I rested my cheek on the mattress. Closed my eyes, felt for my rosary and chanted again and again, 'Holy Mary, mother of God pray for us sinners....' I was becalmed.

Keeping my eyes closed I thought of the past and let images of happier times fill my aching head. Colourful pictures tumbled one after another, like clouds scurrying across the sky. How handsome and athletic Henry had been as he had stood beside me on our wedding day. How we'd love to dance the Volta, Henry's favourite, and that his motto at the jousts, had been, "Sir Loyal Heart". My thoughts moved on to the time we had studied astronomy together with the great Thomas More, for we had both been eager for knowledge.

The birth of our first born son was etched in my memory especially the moment when Henry took our baby into his arms and whispered to him that one day he would be King and I knew in that moment that I could never feel happier or more fulfilled. I was married to the man I loved and we had a son. Such happy memories.

But then anguish as I recalled that after only fifty-seven days our baby, our wondrous creation died. I was bereft. I had failed. I was depressed and distraught because it was my fault, something lacking in me. I relived those terrible times when miscarriage followed miscarriage and I saw again and again the empty look of despair in my husband's eyes. Sometimes I had sensed that he couldn't bear to look at me, as if I was distasteful to him, and the unspoken words of "failure, failure" reverberated in my head, as I watched my ladies in waiting remove the evidence of yet another dead baby.

These thoughts overwhelm me. They are as vivid as if they were happening now. The pain is as deep as before. A terrifying fear is consuming me, I'm becoming unbalanced. Insane. I scream, it is my only outlet, I am like a hunted stag, being pursued by merciless men, who with powerful cross-bows launch arrow after arrow until their prey is reduced to a heap of thudding heart-beats. Slumped on the grass. And is no more. I lie slumped on my bed, my heart reverberating through my body.

'How can that trollop Anne Boleyn know of the love I have and always will have for my husband? Maria, Maria, please help me, I'm going over everything again, and again.'

'What is it my Queen? Calm yourself drink this potion of herbs, it will help you and then we will pray together.'

'Never leave me Maria, my faithful Maria, for I know for certain, that I will be banished and never, never see my Mary, my daughter again. I cannot keep torturing myself. Can anything be more cruel than separating a mother from her child? What is to become of me? Where will they send me?'

Dark, damp, dismal, depressing are the marshes that surround Kimbolton Castle, my prison. I succumb again and again to fevers and chest infections. Bouts of coughing disturb my sleep and I rarely leave my room, my life is devoted to prayer, and celebrating Mass three times a day.

My faithful Maria is always there to comfort me when black bouts of depression overwhelm me. Occasionally I walk outside, but only when a few rays of sun creep along the stone walls and bring some light and just a little warmth into my crumbling prison. On these days I walk with Maria in the knot garden where herbs for soups and potions are grown. But always the mosses and wetness are ready to overtake the little plot.

One rare, warm sunny day, we have a picnic. I reminisce. 'Maria this reminds me of the wonderful picnics we had after a hart had been netted or shot. Such happy memories. Then when we'd get back, I would tell Mary about the hunt and promise that one day she would accompany us. And she'd clap her hands and laugh merrily.'

Tears fall from my eyes, as thoughts of unfulfilled dreams and hopes overcome me, and I feel again the searing pain of a mother, who is separated from her beloved child.

'My Queen, try only to remember the happy times. Remember that the Holy Mother of God is looking over your beloved daughter Mary. Do we not pray for her every day? Have faith my Queen.'

Tasty Persuasions

I am on a mission, not a military one of course, but one just as important. In fact to contemplate failure is out of the question, for the alternative is terrifying. So it's to the cookery books. I have a shelf full. Chinese cooking by Ken Hom, Jamie's Thirty Minute Meals and Nigella's Scrumptious Suppers. My choice is unlimited. But which holds the key to success? Certainly Jez likes food. He enjoys his meals. Occasionally, he enters the kitchen, but always says,

'This is your domain Suze, you're queen of the cooker.'

It's a sign that he's hungry. But which food will make my request irresistible? Victory assured? Will it be sweet ginger chicken and rice? Or Thai-style meat balls? A spicy goulash? Or a Sicilian pasta sauce of tomatoes garlic and almonds? I am a versatile cook, although I say it myself, and would not announce it to the world. I know I can make a success of any of these dishes. In fact that might be one reason why Jez is attracted to me. In fact I'm depending on it. Decision made.

The menu will have an Italian theme. Jez loves the pot-pourri of Mediterranean smells, the sweetness of tomato and basil contrasting with the pungency of garlic. All his taste buds are set alight when he imagines the succulent layers of pasta, sauce, mozzarella and grated parmesan, merging together into forkfuls of delight. As he opens the front door and is confronted with these savoury greetings.

He'll shout, 'Smells as if it's the Verdicchio tonight.'

But unfortunately Jez and I have a big problem. I want to start a family. He doesn't. So now you can probably guess why I'm pulling out all the stops, as they say. We've had argument after argument.

'We're fine as we are,' he'd say and then in his cajoling voice, as if trying to persuade a little girl to eat cabbage, 'there'll be no more surprise trips to Paris, Rome or Morocco. Are you prepared to give up our freedom and exchange all our little treats for sleepless nights and dirty nappies?'

Our future depends on this meal and that's no exaggeration. Time is ticking away, and although sometimes the gnawing feelings would pass, the next day they would be back as disturbing as ever. Breathe deeply and imagine a positive outcome. I repeat my mantra, 'I am determined, I am strong, I am successful.'

Marble surfaces and stainless steel reflect my face. It has a stony look. My eyes set and staring. In fact even non-observant Jez might have detected that there is a change in my usual agreeable, smiling demeanour.

Chopping begins. I find it therapeutic. Cloves of garlic and onion become minute cubes and torn basil leaves are tossed into the terra-cotta pot, followed shortly by tomato purée, salsa and a tin of tomatoes. Special ingredients of mine are a swirl of red wine, a crumbled stock cube and a sprinkle of sugar. Let this scarlet mixture simmer slowly until its dense and will coat every layer of pasta. Sliced mozzarella and grated parmesan will complete the dish.

Pouring myself a Campari and orange I settle myself on the cream cushioned kitchen stool and enjoy this culinary world of senses. Smooth. Savoury. Juicy. Herby. Here I'm in charge, I'm powerful. It's a wonderful feeling. Will Jez be prepared to give all this up, in exchange for bar snacks, pizzas and fries? We'll have to see.

I realise that there have been the unspoken sentences. The silences when the million dollar question could have been voiced, but for fear of a miserable evening, the question never asked. That is over. The campaign has begun. I'm not sure what has given me such determination, perhaps it's phrases like, 'You only have one life, this is not a rehearsal.'

Or the sight of that mother in the park today, laughing with her little girl and doing roly-polies on the grass. The nerves in my stomach are writhing like a nest of baby snakes and remain in a painful spasm. Strategy is becoming action. Tonight there will be confrontation. Whatever the outcome, and no matter how persuasive and appealing the tone of voice. I will remain firm. Surrender, out of the window.

The avenue is quiet. Spindly branches of the laburnum tree move to and fro in the coldish breeze, and there's the ginger cat padding down our path. Thank goodness, he's not paused to mark his territory near my privet bush. Then on the dot. It's six o'clock.

'I think it smells as though it's Verdicchio night tonight,' Jez's voice stops my perusing and I shout, 'Spoken like a true wine-buff'.

He dashes into the kitchen for the corkscrew, gives me a kiss, and dashes out again.

'Buon Appetito, amore mio.'

'Thank you, kind sir,' chinking my glass with his. Jez's plate is scraped until the white pottery is glistening. After relishing the coffee-flavoured creamy Tiramisu, Jez relaxes. He looks so replete, so content. It seems cruel to spoil the moment. But no, this time I am resolute. No sugary phrases are going to win me over.

Tossing and turning internally I begin.

'I have to talk'

He looks up and stares stonily.

'Oh no, not babies again. Are you trying to spoil the evening?'

'No.' The churning in my stomach is almost unbearable. 'No, this is an ultimatum.'

19

'An ultimatum?' Jez says warily.

'I've been your wife now, for eight years and I'm thirty-two. Don't try to interrupt! Listen!' I grip the sides of my chair with trembling fingers.

'I would like to have a baby. I need to have a baby. If a baby is not on your agenda, not part of your plans, then tell me.'

Silence. I twist my emerald engagement ring round and round. As I wait, I reflect on my surprise trips to exotic places. The gifts of jewellery. The bouquets of red roses. But I wait. Jez clears his throat. I haven't actually had to voice the consequences. He understands.

'I suppose I've been a selfish git, wanting you all to myself, not wanting to share you, not even with our baby.'

I thrill when I hear him saying, 'our baby', and have the urge to rush round the table to hug him. But I restrain myself. I have to hear more.

'Do you really agree to starting a family?'

'I do. And by the way, how can I possibly survive without the sumptuous dishes that emerge from our kitchen, like rabbits from a conjuror's hat?'

He hugs me and whispers,' Do you think I could possibly look towards the future, without you.... or your cooking?' He adds with a grin.

I reach for the cafetière and pour us both a strong coffee accompanied by our favourite liqueur, Limoncello. I produce a plate of macaroons. Almond crispiness in one bite. Irresistible....'Like a tasty persuasion?'

Darkness and Light

Here she is sitting in The Town Restaurant wondering how to spend the day. Retirement proving to be lonely and bleak. Audrey yearned to be back again in the midst of the frenzied excitement of school. She grieved the loss of her status as head of the English department. Miss Watkinson's opinion had mattered. Not a book was read without her approval. She forced herself to withdraw from these regrets and dragged her mind back to today, to now. All the self-help books advised that the present moment is the only one we have, but damned hard to realise. Cynthia would be appearing shortly. A routine had emerged, lunch every Wednesday.

'Hello Audrey, sorry I'm late. Missed the bus,' gasped Cynthia.

'Regular occurrence, must do better,' Audrey intonated in a school-teacher voice, whilst pouring Earl Grey tea from a rose decorated tea-pot.

'How are you?' asked Cynthia, as she removed her beige anorak and beige scarf, 'done anything exciting this week?'

'Not really,' Audrey replied, 'aqua aerobics a disaster, a not to be repeated event. I emerged with viola tinted legs and wet hair. The director of operations was wearing pink Lycra. Played loud music and would not have known if I had succumbed to a watery grave.'

Digesting this volley of facts, along with her roast lamb dinner, Cynthia not really knowing what to say, stated the obvious.

'Aqua aerobics isn't your scene then?'

Silence. Cynthia was thinking. Audrey was envying all the people in the restaurant. All the people passing by. All the waitresses. Everybody, who seemed to be having a better time than her. They sat, each lost in their own thoughts, inhaling meaty aromas, until Cynthia ventured to say,

'I know what you will enjoy, and will stimulate the little grey cells. Joining a class at the W.E.A.'

So art appreciation it was. Audrey was invigorated by the information and classroom chat that emanated from the lessons about the lives and paintings of Renoir, Monet and Degas. They seemed to have enjoyed quite decadent lives .The subject absorbed her and Cynthia noticed a transformation in her friend's demeanour and conversation.

Every Wednesday, Audrey regaled Cynthia, with all the facts about the impressionist painters and their works. She was becoming more and more immersed in the subject, noting the colours, that were used to invoke a variety of emotions. Sepia black, burnt umber, intimating dark hidden areas, whilst yellow ochre and lemony tones could suggest sun light and brightness.

Audrey had always been a conscientious worker and now was giving all her energies to the Art Appreciation class. She was looking forward to the visit, to the National, in London, where there was to be an exhibition of impressionism. The group were to travel down to London, by train, and then after the visit meet up for a meal. Audrey approved of these arrangements as she would be able to move around the paintings at her own speed, and really absorb them. Her first visit to a proper exhibition was to be savoured and absorbed, like the first snowdrops in her garden, or the view of hills stretching away to meet a vast blue sky.

Outside the gallery, Audrey marvelled at the sculpture of Nelson, poised high on his column. Standing watch over Trafalgar Square, alive with tourists, which, from his height, must look like scurrying ants.

Before climbing the steps, Audrey paused to admire the impressive colonnades, guarding the entrance of the stone building, and then again, to read the words on an eye-catching poster. "Light is not a thing that can be reproduced, but something that has to be represented with something else with colours." Paul Cezanne .

She pondered, and realised that such a fact had never struck her before, but yes it was true, the statement was thought provoking. Armed with more knowledge she determined to notice the areas of light in the paintings.

Had Degas, one of her favourites, mastered the skill of painting light?

She would soon be discovering the answer to her question, even if she was an unpractised art critic. No one else was in the room, just she and Degas. Good.

Audrey perched on one of the brown, leather seats that were placed at just the right distance, to view the paintings. She had learned that Degas' name was linked with that of paintings of ballerinas. He showed dancers rehearsing and off stage, not just performing before an audience. 'The Dancer at Rest,' caught her eye. The young dancer looked weary and yet relaxed with her curved pose, but central to the picture was the biggest brightest turquoise bow, which contrasted so effectively with her gauzy dress.

Before studying more paintings, Audrey went in search of a café. She needed some sustenance before viewing her favourite painting entitled 'Absinthe'. She'd seen it in a book, it had intrigued her.

As she sipped the latte, realisation dawned. She could do anything she wished. She was her own master. The years of daughterly docility were gone. Her father had always insisted that she chose 'bread and butter subjects' to study, 'none of these wishy washy ones like art or music.'

She had always bowed to his authority, and although she had enjoyed her teaching career, it had been made clear that there was no other choice to be considered. She just had to acquiesce. But now she was in London, drinking coffee in the National, and about to return to the delights of Degas. Freedom was dawning.

When she returned someone else was there, but he was engrossed in 'Absinthe', and didn't even glance towards her. She took up her position and gazed intently at the painting of the woman and her companion.

'Fascinating painting', the man stated, as if he was speaking to someone he knew. 'What a pair. The man, black-suited and black bearded, such a contrast to the cream top and mustard-yellow ruffle that skims over the woman's hollow chest Yet even those colours don't alleviate her dejection do they?'

'No,' replied Audrey, sensing an interesting chat was to ensue about her favourite artist, 'even though she is illuminated in a shaft of bright light. Her unseeing eyes, expressionless face, her woeful demeanour is depicted wonderfully.'

'That's a woman who doesn't care, she's been injured in some way.' As he spoke he stood up and offered his hand. 'Colin Westfield, amateur in art appreciation.'

'Audrey Watkinson, lovely to chat with an admirer of Degas.'

Audrey sensed his sympathy towards this lifeless human-being, a sympathy that she felt. Hadn't she felt lonely, helpless and wretched, just a few months ago? She detached herself from these thoughts and said,

'Does the glass of Absinthe, hold a clue?'

'Probably,' he replied. 'I read that it was called the Green Fairy and was a highly alcoholic aniseed flavoured drink.'

'It was very addictive, and could cause hallucinations', added Audrey. 'It certainly seems that the lady in the painting is under the spell of the green fairy.'

They scrutinised the painting again, commenting, that the light was merciless in its depiction of the two figures. Degas had not let her down.

After a wander around the visitors' centre, they left the gallery together. Audrey to join her group and Colin to catch his train to Birmingham.

'Enjoyed our chat about the paintings,' he said.

Audrey smiled at him, 'Me too, I've really enjoyed the day.'

'Here's a post card of your favourite painting,' he was saying. Then with a wave he was down the steps to join the scurrying ants, an army of nameless people intent on fulfilling their own destinies.

Feelings of elation and emptiness whirled deep inside her as she fingered the card. It was the first time a man had given her a gift. She contemplated again the dejection of the woman in the painting and felt at one with her.

She turned the card over and read:

'colinwestfield@talktalk.net'.

How the Mighty Have Fallen

Connie, courthouse cleaning lady, in fact cleaner extraordinaire, shuffled from room to room. She shuffled because her bunions were hurting, so she wore camel coloured knitted bootees that caused no pressure whatsoever on the offending bones.

No one paid much attention to her as she slipped along the corridors and into meeting-rooms, where she polished and scoured, seemingly so intent on her task that she was unaware of anything but wood, brass and glass. The only clue to Miss Connie's presence were wafts of soap and bleach that emanated from her long rusty cardigan, which was weighed down by over-filled pockets, whose contents bore witness to Connie's state of health. Rennies and Eucalyptus pastilles were ever present, their wrappings sticking to dusters, glasses and keys.

But our silent worker had hearing as sharp as a fox, and so learned many secrets about the citizens of Edendale. These stories to her were more nutritious than food, more enjoyable than the whiskey and ginger that she drank each night. And as her needles clicked, she savoured the knowledge that she had gleaned that day. After all she reasoned there hadn't been much excitement in her life.

Her mother had treated her like a skivvy. She'd been at the beck and call of her four brothers. No one had noticed her unhappiness. No one had ever afforded her any attention, except to order her to wash the pots, peel the 'taters, make a cuppa, do an errand. Now she was important and had nuggets of information.

'Fancy Peter Reynolds buying knackered race horses and selling them to Watson's the butcher's,' she said in shocked tones, to Millie the post-mistress.

'Them folks who live in big houses, and dress in them designer clothes 'ave always got something to 'ide.'

'Are you sure?' Millie the postmistress said in a whisper, 'How do you know?'

'Oh I heard the flower arrangers in church talking.'

Happy and fulfilled Connie marched along, feelings of jubilation, overcoming painful feet. Head held high. Eyes alert. Chiselled nose ready for more foraging, and forage it did into the misdemeanours of others. A well-honed skill.

Where else could she scatter her seeds? If she had unfulfilled dreams and hopes why shouldn't others suffer? Particularly those that sped by in cherry-red sports cars or strode along the High Street in high-heeled shoes swinging big leather hand bags.

Connie had never had a new hand bag, always from a charity shop. She noticed hand bags. Fashionable. Shiny. In bright yellow, purple and pillar-box red, Connie's favourite. But as her mother used to say when she'd ventured to ask for something,

'I'm afraid you'll have to want.'

As she passed Watson's, she noticed that the butcher's striped blind was down and in the window, CLOSED TILL FURTHER NOTICE.

"How the mighty have fallen," Connie thought, one of her favourite phrases, and felt such a sense of satisfaction and importance that everything else faded. She flourished, blossomed, on the sins of others convinced that she was justified in her thoughts and actions.

She was not to realise however that her days as a "spy exceptional" were drawing to a close.

Although she did have time to spread the news that 'The posh bloke at the bungalow had been caught speeding and had lost his licence for a year,' adding jokingly, 'You might see him at the bus stop!'

And that Mrs. Stuck-up Smedley-Jones had had one over the eight and had had to be accompanied home by the police.

However a few weeks later a little while after the Smedley-Jones event she was asked to go to the main office. Mr Rathbone the chief man was at his desk. Familiar wafts of soapiness and bleach heralded Connie's arrival. Dressed in her striped jumper, that yelled thrift and her olive-green skirt that lapped the edges of her bootees, she entered the room. A hand knitted person. Bobbing slightly in deference to her boss.

'Sit down Connie,' Mr Rathbone said in a friendly voice, as he shuffled through some papers. His stomach felt queasy as he asked, 'How are you today?'

'All right thank you Mr. Rathbone.' She twisted the duster into a plait and sat uneasily, enclosed in the scrolled oak chair.

'I've just finished polishing the brass handles on the Court doors, they're shining like....' Connie paused searching desperately for the words to describe how bright they were.

'I'm sure they are. We've never had a more diligent cleaner than you. But I'm afraid,' he paused, as if gathering courage, 'that we're going to have to cut down on staff, due to....'

'What?' she blurted out, her crumpled demeanour suddenly at attention. Alert. Wary. What did he mean? He can't be sacking me. Heart thumping. Pulse racing. Hot. Cold. She held the edges of her cardigan, and studied the floor. Tiles that she'd polished week after week.

Mr. Rathbone's voice became comforting, as if he understood all about Connie's life and feelings.

'Of course you can work another week and then probably you'll be able to find some other employment. I, of course will give you a superb reference and we shall have a farewell party for you,' he added in a cheerful tone.

That night Connie could not sleep. She saw herself as a nobody again. Alone and lonely, with no interesting tit-bits of gossip to tell. Her status as a cleaner at the courthouse vanquished. She had rarely been troubled by conscience but there was an insistent voice inside her that perhaps, just perhaps, Mr, Rathbone had some inkling about her after work schedule.

Not even the thought of a party could cheer her up. What would she wear?

The farewell lasted only half an hour. She'd managed to find a maroon jacket with a velvet collar, that had been her mother's and she'd bought a pair of mottled sandals from a bargain shop. The only problem was that her bunions sprouted between the straps, like mature onions. The pièce de resistance was a pair of pearl earrings. Mr. Rathbone presented her with a voucher for £100 to be spent at Debenham's.

Connie walked slowly along the High Street, taking no pleasure in seeing Mrs. Smedley-Jones waiting at the bus stop. It gave her no satisfaction. She felt guilty when the lady, who she'd judged to be too stuck up, smiled at her and asked if she felt OK.

Her home had an aura of brownness shrouded in a layer of dust. Connie neglected her own surroundings, they held a legion of miserable memories. As she sat in the cracked vinyl chair and listened to next door's dog barking, she fingered the voucher and fought to imagine herself with a big, bright chrome-studded handbag.

Uncomfortable and despondent feelings continued to circle in Connie's mind, pricking her innards.

These wonderings tortured her. Destroyed her sleep and made her head throb. Then after days of exhaustion and self-questioning, a phrase of her mother's emerged, "I've not killed anybody 'ave I?" and with that thought in mind Connie began to recover.

Swinging the geranium red bag Connie made her way down the High Street and turned into the "Hottye Pye Shoppye," where she placed herself in the window and ordered a pot of tea. She was feeling much better and had decided that everyone could make mistakes, and that she would confess her sins, not in too much detail, but sufficiently to gain forgiveness.

Besides she had heard that the cleaner at the vicarage was giving up, due to ill-health.

Unexpected Joy

Christmas Eve! Jenny placed the last shimmering bauble onto the bushy little Christmas tree, the spicy smell of pine filling her nostrils. Usually she enjoyed the ritual of decorating, but this year it had been a chore. She'd always been a 'buxom wench,' as Malcolm laughingly described her, but she seemed to piling on weight so rapidly that every bend and stretch, was an effort. The wooden sledges and dolls bought at Lincoln Market had evoked the usual happy memories but as her fingers caressed the cherub faced baby Jesus her eyes filled with tears.

Despairingly she sat down and eyed the sitting room. Once it had seemed very important to choose the right shade of beige carpet to contrast with the leaf sprigged settee, but now it seemed very unimportant. She sighed and began to reason with herself, as she had done many times before.

'I've got a faithful and adoring husband. We're both healthy. I have a lovely mother and good friends.... but....'she stopped. It was too painful to carry on....

Glancing in the circular mirror that adorned one of the alcoves, she could see her face was pale and puffy. Her engagement ring was biting into her flesh. Easing it off her finger she thought of that summer evening twenty-two years ago when Malcolm had fumbled in his pocket and produced a midnight-blue satin box. Two years later they had married. Proudly Dad had escorted her to the church, that was only across the road and she in her cream silk wedding dress had gripped his arm nervously. She'd had so many dreams and plans.... but....

'I'm home,' Malcolm's cheery voice from the hall, brought her back to reality.

'Shepherd's pie in the oven.' she called.

'Great, 'cos this shepherd's famished.'

He usually was, when he came home from work.

Slowly Jenny went into the kitchen, transformed by her husband from a dark, poky, little room into a show piece. He had extended the walls and lined them with tall white cupboards contrasting well with mottled grey worktops. She'd added artistic touches of her own, colourful ceramic plates, reminders of holidays in Spain and Tunisia. Potted ferns cascaded over the glistening white tiles, like emerald green fountains.

Jenny ran her fingers through Malcolm's dark wiry curls as he hungrily ate the gravy soaked potato.

'Smashing, my compliments to the chef,' he said.

'Thank you sir. Malc, I'm feeling so tired, I'm going to have an early night.'

Immediately Jenny felt Malcolm's concern.

'What's wrong love?'

'Just feeling weary, I'm going to bed so that I can enjoy tomorrow.'

'OK. Don't forget that Father Christmas will be coming to good little girls.'

'Oh don't remind me,' said Jenny, with tears running down her face.

Malcolm sighed as he watched Jenny's hunched shoulders. He always seemed to be saying the wrong thing. He was pondering about Jenny's crying, when his thoughts were interrupted by a frenzied shout. He leapt up the stairs and saw that Jenny was in pain.

'Ring for the doctor Malc. I'm getting gripping cramping pains in my back.'

'Doctor, Doctor Khacem can you come quick, my wife's in terrible pain,' Malcolm stammered down the phone.

'Who is your wife? And where do you live?' the doctor asked calmly.

'Jennifer Harrison, and we live at 17, Shakespeare Street, New Houghton.'

'I'll come now, Mr. Harrison.'

Dr. Khacem recognised fear. She also knew that the Harrisons rarely came to the surgery and would not have telephoned on Christmas Eve unless it was an emergency. She drove along the illuminated streets, bright with multi-coloured lights and prancing reindeer that had glowing red noses. As she got out of her car she looked up at a huge silver star on the Church Spire. Its beams proclaiming Christmas.

After a quick examination of Jenny, the doctor said, 'You're about to have a baby. Didn't you realise you were expecting?'

'No, I.... after twenty years of marriage I'd given up hope and at forty-two I never dreamed that I would ever have a baby, and I haven't attended any ante-natal classes or been checked for anything. Doctor will the baby be all right ?'

'You will be fine, let's concentrate on bringing this baby into the world.'

Paints a Thousand Words

Packing finished at last. I'm preparing for the holiday of a lifetime. One of those Imaginative Adventure Holidays to the Pacific Coast of America. I've checked the documents time and time again, passport, boarding pass, ticket, credit, debit cards and some dollars. I recite the list like a mantra. One of my biggest fears is arriving at the Airport without my passport! Now departure date is drawing near I keep getting mixed feelings of excitement and apprehension. Hope I'll like the other members of the group.

My real worry is Gran, my comforter, my best friend. She's become forgetful and now lives in a care home and doesn't get out much, and won't have any visitors whilst I'm away. Mum is too wrapped up in herself and gone to live with her latest partner.

When I was young I'd call on Gran every day, after school, to have tea. I always preferred to be with her than to be at home.

She'd say, 'Come and see my new rockery plants.' I can still remember their names; saxifrage, snow in summer, floribunda, starburst and so on.

'Let's go for a walk in the woods,' she would suggest, knowing how much I enjoyed picking a small bunch of bluebells, or searching for shiny chestnuts, eating juicy blackberries. We were always on the lookout for a new bird, both equipped with binoculars so that we could see every detail on even the smallest wren.

Another hobby of Gran's was oil painting, her arthritic hands manipulating the finest brush. On my eighteenth birthday she gave me a framed painting showing a bird emerging from a river, wings outstretched, feathers glistening with beads of water, its profile hawk-like, and its catch, shiny, slippery and grey.

'It's wonderful. What kind of bird is it?'

We were sitting in the garden, surrounded by flowers. The fragrance of the roses was almost as pleasurable as the chocolate aromas from my birthday cake.

'It's an osprey,' she announced proudly, 'a rare sight in this country now, but they can be seen easily in Canada and North America. It's one of few birds in the world that can catch live fish with its talons'.

I studied each brushstroke on the birds wings and was amazed how Gran had caught the brightness of its eye and curve of its beak.

'I'd love to see one in action wouldn't you Gran?'

'Me too.' she said. 'But Canada's rather a long way away.'

'Better win the lottery and we could take a trip across the pond.'

'Well you never know our luck,' said Gran, her eyes sparkling. She often had an impish air about her.

When I moved from home into my own flat, she'd inquired, if I'd taken the osprey painting with me, I'd assured her that wherever I lived, the osprey would be with me.

When Mum had seen it she'd said, 'What's so special about a bird with a fish? I wouldn't give it house-room. You never did have any taste. You don't take after me at all.'

The group I meet at Manchester Airport are a cheerful bunch and by the time I arrive at Seattle I feel confident that I'm in for a good trip with like-minded people. Camper vans are to be our transport, with our own drivers. Talk about well-equipped, they had every mod-con.

Our first journey takes us to the Olympic National Park where there are the tallest trees I've ever seen. Not isolated giants but in huge groups, and yet overpowering them all is Mount Olympus, with its snowy peaks sharply contrasting with the cornflower blue sky.

Rain forests are eerie places with ferns covering the ground, giving a primeval atmosphere. Greyish green mosses drip in festoons from the trees and ghostly finger-like lichens hang from every branch. These forests demand silence.

If a bird is heard we freeze and scan the trees and bushes. Red-winged blackbirds and fat American robins, become commonplace.

One morning, just before we are due to return home, we are travelling beside the Columbia river when I shout, 'STOP! I've seen an Osprey.' I had just spotted its white head above an untidy nest of twigs, constructed on top of a navigational light. Cameras immediately at the ready, we eye the osprey with intent, like cats stalking a bird. Suddenly it stands, grey sturdy legs supporting its grey and white feathered body, eyes beady and unblinking. Rising into the air, the osprey scans the water, plunges and emerges triumphant with a big fish held firmly in its spiky padded feet. Silence, as we absorb the amazing spectacle that we have witnessed.

A birthday present given some years ago, flashes into my mind and along with it a picture of Gran, frail and diminished, sitting quietly, hoping someone will wheel her into the garden. How we'd joked about a trip over the pond to see an osprey. Now I had, and every detail of its fishing prowess had been caught on camera.

Now I really wanted to return home, it was as if a mission had been accomplished.

A few days later, I visit Gran, yes there she is enveloped in a high-backed armchair, the only words being spoken are those of the commentator on television. No one seems to be watching or listening.

'Gran would you like to go into the garden?' She nods. So off we go. I often wonder if she remembers me and our happy times together. I chat on and on, pointing out carnations, lobelia, snap dragons. I wheel her near an arch-way of roses and let her inhale their fragrance, it seems to energise her and she smiles. I wonder if it stirs something in her mind that is lying just beyond her grasp.

Back in her room, drinking tea, I tell her about my holiday. I don't know if she is understanding me or not. I produce my photographs. They are excellent, so vivid and detailed.

Gran takes the photographs one by one and studies them intently, particularly that of the osprey emerging from the water, wings outstretched, talons extended. Holding its magnificent catch. She traces her finger over the outline of the bird. Looking up at me she smiles and strokes my hand. And there just might be.... a slightly impish gleam in her eye as she whispers,

'Our Osprey.'

It Could Have Been Worse

Had a bad day today. Got to share it with someone. Anyone in fact. It started OK.

Morning sunshine promising all things good. Yellowness everywhere, forsythia a fitting background to golden yellow daffodils. I pick up the Slimmer's Supreme booklet, it is my constant companion. Yes breakfast will be a poached egg on toasted granary bread, followed by grapes.

Poaching eggs, I hoped would be a culinary success, as I have purchased some rubber cup shapes from Betterware, which will float on steaming water and produce the perfect poached eggs. I could hardly wait to reach such perfection in the kitchen world. Full of confidence I stride into the kitchen, dressing gown sleeves rolled up to the elbow. Oil the rubber cup and crack an egg. Disaster! Raw egg flows over the warm ceramic hob immediately transforming itself into a crackly cellophane look alike. Ten minutes later after an energetic rub the hob looks presentable again. But still an empty rubber cup. Try again but this time the procedure is accomplished over a work surface and magically an egg is lying oh so beautifully in the centre of the hallowed cup. Meanwhile water is steaming in the prepared vessel, I lower the egg slowly and tenderly into the saucepan, and put on the lid. After a few minutes I gingerly remove the lid to have a peep, horror of horrors the rubber cup has been torpedoed and a cloud of congealed egg white is swirling around uncontrollably. Horrible words escape from my lips, as I dash the pan's contents into the sink and with a swift movement turn the pan upside down on the draining board, rubber cup and all. The words in the catalogue dance before my eyes, 'Impossible to fail, perfect poached eggs every time.'

The Slimmer's Supreme booklet, catches my eye, that deserves incarceration and the photograph of a very fat woman adorning the fridge is torn from its cellophane hinges. I scour the forbidden drawer. There lurking in hidden depths. Underneath a healthy food booklet is, wonder of wonders.... a giant Mars Bar. I tenderly turn down the paper just half way, my intention being to consume just half. The first bite is wonderful. My mouth is a mix of milk chocolate, soft fudge and liquid caramel. Soon the whole bar has disappeared, as if by magic, and I'm licking the strings of caramel that are clinging to the wrapper, soon the wrapper is devoid of stickiness and it is hurled into the bin.

Perhaps it will be a poached egg tomorrow.

I am hoping that the rest of the day will go without a hitch. I suddenly decide that I'll go to town, well after half past nine the silver-surfers can travel gratis. The bus is quite full, the first free one always is. Oh no, I'm sitting by Olive again, by the time I get to town, I will be well informed of all her ailments, from her head to her bunions. Her opening line is, 'My chest's not very good, I'm a bit wheezy, got to use my inhalers.'

'Oh dear,' I say.

'And my stomach's playing up, been taking Gaviscon by the bucketful. And my knees, can't describe the pain.'

'Not often you're short of words.' I manage to utter and so interrupt the medical flow.

'You'd think I'd got shares in Fiery Jack, you have to be careful to wash your hands after applying that stuff. 'Cos if its rubbed into the wrong part you'll know about it.'

An image of Fiery Jack coming into contact with any tender part of the body, makes me cringe. But I've taken seriously Olive's advice to place Fiery Jack and haemorrhoid ointment well apart in the medicine cabinet.

I need therapy, my favourite clothes shop is there waiting to calm me. Roman Originals, " by any other name would smell as sweet". After trying on many jackets, some flowery, some covered in bright geometric shapes, I settle for a navy and white spotted creation, with a slightly flared hem that flows over my derrière wondrously. Only thirty pounds, a real bargain.

'Horror of Horrors,' the second time I've uttered those words today, I've changed handbags, no card. Only two pound coins in the side pocket. I watch, red faced as the jacket re-emerges from its wrapping and with profuse apologies, I step into the street feeling insecure and quite bereft. I purchase a Mars bar, I need sugar so that I don't collapse. I then realise I can't even buy a cup of coffee, I need caffeine to sustain me. Then a brainwave, they know me so well in the local branch of the Halifax, they might lend me twenty pounds.

The bank clerk is asking me about my pass words, I can't remember which favourite colour I'd given back in the mists of time, or which of our dogs' names I have chosen, in fact my mind is totally blank. I feel like a con woman. Then the heavens are smiling on me, I spy a youth, whom I have taught, behind the counter. He verifies that I am Mrs. Robertson, and that I was his teacher. I emerge with a twenty pound note. Have a double shot espresso, and am now over brimming with caffeine and pulsating like a reverberating drum. I decide to return home.

Oh no, there's my neighbour approaching. She's always immaculate. Hair glossy. Face made up perfectly. No lines around eyes. No red veins on cheeks. Smart suit emphasising her neat little rump and she's managing to balance on 'to die for' shoes that match her black glossy handbag.

I on the other hand am wearing trousers with the sewn in pleat, a beige anorak topped with a flushed face, and a chin that sports a few sprouting white hairs. I'm definitely in 'the old trout' group. But I conjure up a smile. We exchange a few polite words and then I explain that I am in a hurry, got to get to the doctors for my M.O.T. Actually that is true, although I had almost forgotten because of the poached egg disaster, so I turn into the doctors, wondering what effect the big injection of caffeine will have had on my blood pressure ratings.

It's sky high and then horror of horrors, third time today, forgotten the urine sample. I'm instructed to go and produce a few drops. Have you ever had to perform by instruction? I succeed and present a minute amount of liquid, but am told that it probably will be sufficient.

I emerge from the surgery feeling that I have failed in the culinary area, in the financial planning area and in the medical area. I therefore must be a hundred per cent failure, so I'll just stop trying so hard and like the sensible woman in Pam Ayres poem, become "An old trout and let it all sprout".

But tomorrow's another day isn't it? Better go and rescue the Supreme Slimmer's Guide from the dustbin!

A Watery Grave

'I'm glad you've discovered me!' he shouted, 'I'm Private George Hewitt of the Lancashires.' His words tumbling out as if he was fearful that I would swim away.

I'm amazed and shocked, and yet instinctively I swim towards the voice.

He continues to shout, 'I was puzzled by your outfit, but now I realise you're a diver. Are you searching for the remnants of war? You'll find plenty of those around here.'

'Yes.... I dive here often'.... I manage to answer.... 'looking for the rusty, remains of the Gallipoli Campaign.' A weird realisation begins to surface in my brain.

Private Hewitt lives here in the deep waters of the Dardanelles. He must have been in these murky depths for about one hundred years surrounded by wreckage. His only company, shoals of little fish darting through waving weeds, and occasionally the sound of muffled voices accompanied by the rhythmic slap of waves against the rocks.

It was surreal. Of course I was astounded, mesmerised, but eager to hear more.

'So have you time to hear my story?' he asked. 'It's a tragic one, but then war is tragic.'

I checked my air supply and settled down as he began, 'It was 1915, when I waded towards the peninsula, I knew very little about the terrain. The top brass said it would be easy, and issued us with hand-drawn maps of the shoreline. As I made my way through the shallow water, I was alert.

Eyes, ears and limbs standing to attention. Every heart beat a thump, which shuddered through my rib cage. Then grating sounds as my boots landed on the shingle, frightening when you're trying to move as silently as a prowling cat. Everywhere was silent, a dark silence. If you can imagine it? And then, all hell was let loose, bullets, like huge raindrops showered down. They'd got machine guns, no mistaking that noise, like the drills I'd used down the pit. I miraculously turned into a dung beetle and burrowed for dear life into the sand. Sand, my only protection. The wonderful plans of the Admiralty hadn't included trenches and hide-outs, but I realised, even in the middle of all this mayhem, they'd be impossible to spot from out at sea. I imagined the Turks, like buzzards, waiting to swoop. But take it from me, when your life's in danger you can move like a machine, even though your heart's thumping, you can dig, fast and deep. It's self-preservation nothing else. My buddies were dying, hundreds of them, easy targets. Just as the saying goes, "like lambs to the slaughter". So we've arrived. Quite a welcoming. The journey from Egypt hadn't been a bed of roses either, a lot of the chaps had been sea-sick, so we'd been looking forward to getting to dry land.

After this first attack, there was a lull. The Turks knew just where we were and were preparing for the next time. So we had to dig trenches as fast as we could.

Skirmishes happened. A successful advance was made. That's when you might think we'd have continued attacking, but no, it seemed that even the officers didn't know what to do. A proper fiasco. Granted the Turks were in a better position, on higher ground and had better views of the land and sea. Of course the idea was to get to Constantinople and be in charge of the Dardanelles. I often wondered if it would ever happen. In fact as the months rolled on, I got to thinking it never would. Sometimes the company would set off and end up lost, or surrounded by the worst barbed wire.

Impossible to cut through. Might be hard to believe,' he gave a wry smile, 'but the Turks' head gear was a fez, even when they were fighting. One of the favourite tricks of the enemy was to plant mines. They'd managed to blow up a number of ships.

But enough of war talk, believe you me, soldiers often think of home. When I was sitting huddled in the trench I often thought of Mary and the kids, Gladys nine and Edgar seven. I pondered hours about their lives, I knew it wouldn't be easy, especially when they got the news that I was never coming back. There wasn't much support for a widow, but I'm talking as though time's stood still. I like to think of them as when I was called up, Edgar had got my looks, fair hair and eyes as blue as a summer sky.

Mary's last words had been "Look after yourself, we'll be waiting for you" and they'd all kissed me. Those kisses.... he paused as he relished the memory. 'I'll never forget them, you see kissing was for special occasions. As I'd set off I wondered, if I'd see our street again, narrow brick houses, white edged door steps, clipped privet hedges. I could smell meat stewing and newly baked bread, mouth-watering memories that travelled with me as I walked across the allotments. A short cut to the railway station. I remember taking in a deep breath, that I swear went from the roots of my hair to the soles of my feet. Then I'd turned for one last look. I wanted to print that scene, onto my mind. It was a view I wanted to carry with me, and then, conjure it up like a magician, pulling yards of hankies out of a hat. 'No more looking back,' I'd muttered and strode towards the unknown.'

'Enough reminiscing of home,' he said, and peered into the waving fronds of the sea-weeds, as if he needed time.... to gain strength.... to carry on.

I never felt that he wanted or needed a comment from me. This was George's story and his alone.

He continued, 'Days, weeks, months pass, often the Turks would throw dates and sweets into no-man's land. We returned their offerings, with tins of beef and cigs. It was good to have a change of diet.

Come August, it was hot, a blazing sun shone down on us all, friend and foe alike. It was relentless. Scorched and blistered, we huddled into any spot of shade we could find.'

'Can you picture what it was like?' he suddenly asked me.

'I'm trying to imagine how terrible it was,' I answered, with sincere feeling, 'but I think you would have to be there to really know.'

He nodded. He seemed to approve of my answer, I sensed that as he told me of all these happenings, it was as if he was shedding a heavy weight, a burden that he'd been carrying all these years.

As he spoke I recognised his anguish, as he described the terrible conditions.

'No toilets, griping pains, incessant diarrhoea. Men dying with dysentery. An explosion of buzzing blue-bottles, landing on every inch of your skin. I remember one chap saying, "It's like living in a midden and an open cemetery". There were so many bodies lying about, bloated, dead meat. When I got the runs, I knew, and said to my buddy,

"Jim if I don't make it, go and see Mary and tell her and the kids that I've thought about them every day, specially at Christmas and on their birthdays, and that I love 'em." Jim just patted me on the back.

During the last days as I got weaker I began to think back over my life, going to school in patched trousers and holes in my boots. I thought a lot about my mam, who was always on duty, washing, scrubbing, baking bread, and then of the terrible day when I'd come home from school, and Dad saying,

"Your mam's gone."

48

"Gone where?" I'd asked.

"She's died".

'I remember rushing outside to the field, where I'd played wondering why it was that my mam had gone and left us with a no-good father. I missed everything about her, her smile, her work-worn hands. She gave us love, something my dad couldn't do. I can tell you, I felt alone.'

George sighed, 'But everything passes. Work was next. Down the pit, but you know there's a lot of joking and miners look out for each other. Then I met Mary, she'd been in service, working as a maid at one of the big houses. We'd courted for about a year and saved enough money to get married and begin a family. They were the best years. Mary was a hard worker and I knew I was a better Dad to Gladys and Edgar than my father had ever been.'

'I've wished many times that I'd been able to go back to them, and have a bit longer on the earth.'

'What do you think this war was about?'

Without waiting for an answer, he said, 'I know, for sure that thousands died, English, Aussies, Turks and Germans. Do you think it was all worth it?'

But again he didn't seem to need an answer. He'd made up his own mind He'd told his story. He seemed to have fulfilled an ambition, satisfied a need and was at peace.

As I swam towards the surface of these rusted waters my head was filled with questions some of which might never be answered.

Had it all been worth it? Had it all been worth it?

Inspired by Rupert Brooke's poem, The Soldier....
    If I should die, think only this of me,
    That there's some corner of a foreign field
    That is forever England. ...

An English Girl Abroad....
Introducing Mamma

'Cento Trento mamma.' Mamma was my mother-in-law, and a wonderful cook. I was her new daughter-in-law, English and unpractised in all culinary skills. Frightening! One hundred and thirty perfectly shaped tortellini were lying like a regiment of well ordered soldiers on white sheets. Drying. Meanwhile a muscle bound hen was simmering in a large terra-cotta pot. A short while ago it had been running free, but then mamma had spotted its plump outline, in an instant it was grabbed, neck twisted and very soon in the pot along with plum tomatoes, basil, onion, garlic, salt, pepper and cooking slowly. First course prepared. There was no fast or frozen food in Mamma's kitchen.

Second course cotelette. I liked cotelette, finely cut slices of veal dipped into beaten eggs and then pressed into bread crumbs and fried. I had accompanied Mamma to the butchers. The Italian queuing system never failed to amaze me. Did I say system? Wrong word. We entered a well shaded shop, the butcher on a raised platform, like a player on a stage.

'Twelve slices of vitello Salvatore,' Mamma yelled, from the back, in her most commanding voice. I knew that veal was being ordered and that it was very tender. Mamma hadn't seemed to notice that the shop was full. I thought someone would object, and say something like, 'Aye there's a queue if you hadn't noticed,' or 'Who do you think you are? Wait your turn,' but nothing was said, and I had to presume that mamma, la Signora, had a reputation. No one knew me, so I wasn't too embarrassed.

Fragrances, sweet and savoury, filled the tiny kitchen, some escaping through the open window into the yard and surrounding apartments. Basil, tomato and meaty scents alerted the taste buds, heralding the promise of delicious food.

A cream cloth, with an ecru crocheted trim adorned the oval table. Eight sparkling glasses were overlooked by two large bottles of fruity red wine. The wine merchant came regularly. He grew the grapes, he harvested them, he made the wine and then delivered it to his faithful customers. I noted that Italians weren't sophisticated about which wine to drink with which food. They recognised a good wine, and drank it. After consuming a few glasses, voices would be raised, hands banged on the table, and when I was new to this happening, I would ask tentatively, 'What's going on?'

'Football,' was the reply.

When everyone was seated, with Papa at the head of the table. Mamma appeared with a huge tureen. Dimpled dumplings bobbed about in herby soup, the aroma wafting around the shaded room, stimulating taste buds. Every mouthful scrumptious, as the melting parmesan made the food more appetizing. If that were possible. When every plate was cleared, an oval pottery dish was placed in the centre of the table covered with crispy cotelette, to be accompanied by a tomato salad and rustic bread, or pane di grano, which a local baker produced. Veal, tomatoes, virgin olive oil and coarse bread, interspersed with full-bodied wine. Food fit for a king.

Would I ever master these culinary skills? I wondered, as I thought of my lack of domesticity. Mine had been an academic schooling with only one year of Domestic Science, when I had produced scones and rock buns. Both had emerged from the oven fairly rocky. So competing with a superb chef like mamma, was going to be some challenge. As the days passed, more and more rapturous feasts emerged from the tiny kitchen, I became certain that Enzo, my new husband, would not be anticipating living on love alone. Disturbing.

Every day I sat in the kitchen with mamma. And a note book. I watched whilst pink hands, chopped, kneaded, moulded, stirred and served. Mamma pausing every now and again to wipe her forehead on her white apron. Kitchen heat and unrelenting sun were not sympathetic companions to cooking. I had to smile to myself, when I remembered the first spaghetti I had cooked. It had emerged from the pan as a glutinous ball, 'al dente'? Not really. The sauce was thin and pooled at the bottom of the bowl. It had no resemblance to mamma's. Hers was a sauce of many flavours, crushed garlic, succulent basil, plum tomatoes and olive oil and then the mixture simmered and simmered until its density was obvious.

Back in England, I tried out my newly learned skills and Enzo would say with a grin, 'Brava, brava, not quite as mamma used to make but a good try.'

I began to include more dishes, pasta fagioli, a tasty and healthy dish with smoked bacon and beans, which became a favourite. Along with cannelloni, past'al forno, roast chicken and potatoes with a good helping of rosemary. I had learned how aromatic herbs made meat, fish, sauces and soups so appetizing.

As the years passed even Enzo enjoyed some English cuisine, roast beef, Yorkshire pud, and gravy. Apple pie, custard, trifle and lemon meringue, were added to our menu.

It's taken some years for me to become confident in my production of Italian dishes. But my, son's favourite is pasta fagioli, and my grandchildren say, 'Grandma's lasagne is the best.' I have shown my daughter-in-law how to make a good sauce, so cooking skills have turned a full circle.

Now when I appear from my kitchen with a big dish of lasagne, and look around the table, I can imagine how mamma had felt. How glad I am, that all those years ago I sat in a little kitchen, with a note book. And will be forever grateful to my hard-working mother-in-law, who introduced me, a fledgling to these wonderful tasty dishes. ....That indomitable little woman.... Mamma.

Behind the Grease Paint

He strode up the winding path, his open ended boots scattering white grit onto the scarlet geraniums, that edged his route to an impressive looking house. He swore under his breath. 'Bloody toffs.'

His black-ringed eyes were alert and bright, red make-up enlarged his lips making them look jolly and smiling, whilst in reality they were thin and disparaging. Yes Charlie, the clown, had mastered the art of make-up. Nobody, particularly children would have come close to him without his liberally applied grease-paint. He was hoping that "the toffs" would have invited lots of children, who would gradually creep closer and closer to him as he performed his tricks.

'Good afternoon Mrs. Pendleton,' was Charlie's greeting as he swept off his tattered bowler hat in a mock bow.

'You're looking lovely today, as you always do. And may I say that flowered dress really suits you.'

Charlie sensed that Mrs. Pendleton didn't really like him, but that she liked leaving him to entertain the children, whilst she slipped into the kitchen for a natter and a coffee.

The children always enjoyed his performances, and within minutes of entering the sitting room, he'd always say, 'Off you go Mrs. Pendleton, these little treasures will be fine with Charlie.'

'Well, you were such a hit with them at the Christmas party, no doubt it will be a repeat performance,' she said, closing the door on the expectant group.

Immediately Charlie went into action, saying, 'I can't hear any cheering for Uncle Charlie.'

The room was soon in uproar, 'Hooray for Uncle Charlie, hooray!'

When seated in front of them, he liked to see their adoring eyes and smell their soapy smooth skin. When he produced items from his pockets he loved to invite Poppy up to find a ball or a flower. He liked to feel her little searching fingers exploring every inch until with glee, she'd shout, 'Found it, found it.'

'My word Poppy, you're a clever little girl. You can sit on my knee, and help me with my next trick.'

Charlie knew where Poppy lived. Not at this house. It was Olivia who lived here, Poppy's best friend. He studied the little girl's comings and goings. Her mother took her and Olivia to school every morning and collected them at home-time. That was the trouble with these posh kids, chauffeured everywhere.

When he'd got home from school his mother would have been spread out in a chair, snoring, a couple of empty wine bottles on the carpet. The sink full of pots, each cup stained brown and each plate bearing witness to greasy fry-ups. If he wanted a drink he would quickly rinse the cup under the cold water and then balance it on top of a tottering pyramid of chipped crockery. Sometimes he would spend a few minutes staring at his mother, thinking what a waste of space she was. That's what his dad called her. It never seemed to dawn on Charlie to criticise his dad. As soon as he'd got to sixteen he'd been sent to a Young Offender's place. He'd liked it there, you got good meals and slept under clean sheets that smelled of a life that Charlie had never known, although he was aware that some people lived in places that didn't pong of unwashed bodies and clothes.

Once he'd delivered newspapers and had caught glimpses of shiny sinks and gleaming tiles as he'd peeped through letter boxes. When he'd come out of the detention centre he'd been wandering round a fair-ground and had been fascinated by a clown juggling with hoops and plates. He'd followed the man to his caravan and waited to see if he was going to do another show, but had been amazed to see the performer re-appear without the orange tufted hair, scarlet cheeks, cherry nose and huge smiling lips. He'd been transformed. The transformation was for the worst. He looked weird, yellow, wrinkled, and miserable. It was a Eureka moment for Charlie, although, he wouldn't have used those precise words. He realised that if this chap could do it then so could he. He could transform himself into a laughing, colourful clown, who would be able get children to come close to him. The next time he got his unemployment money, he would buy some balls and balloons and practise making some balloon animals. He'd always been good with his hands, so his Dad had said

Charlie now applied himself to putting on make-up, practising card tricks, hiding sweets, twisting balloons, popping up his tie and swivelling his button hole so that it squirted water. When he felt that he'd mastered his art, Charlie asked his friend at the hostel to help him write an advert.

INVITE CHARLIE THE CLOWN TO YOUR CHIL-DREN'S PARTY, HE'S AVAILABLE ANY TIME OF THE DAY AND HE'S A STAR! RING.... MOB. 07865175903

He'd placed the advert in burger bars, pizza huts and hairdressing salons. Soon he was receiving bookings. Charlie was glad of the cash. But especially he liked being close to children, whilst despising their parents, who he thought of as lazy buggers, who'd do anything to get their children looked after by anyone but themselves. Charlie nursed a deep hatred against anyone who spoke 'posh' and lived in a big house.

He kept watch on the house where Poppy lived, always hoping to find her on her own, but so far had had no luck. But Charlie had 'stickability'. When he'd left the Young Offenders, they'd written on his report that Charlie could concentrate on a task if he was interested. His Dad had said, "You take after me 'ar Charlie, I can study them 'orses till me 'ead aches."

One afternoon he was wandering near Poppy's house in his full gear when he saw the little girl picking blue-bells at the end of her drive.

'Poppy, it's Charlie, your friend. Shall I help you pick a big bunch of flowers?'

'Hello Charlie,' said Poppy, 'thank you, but mummy said only pick a few it's not right for c... conser... vation to gather huge bunches.'

Charlie seething with rage and frustration, had been hoping to lure the little girl across the road and into the woods. Underneath his breath he was mimicking the little girls words. 'Mummy says this and mummy says that.'

His own mother hadn't cared where he'd gone or who'd he been with. He'd earned a tenner or two when he'd let a queer chap called Frank take some photos of him. Not that he wanted to hurt Poppy. In fact he wanted to stroke her and let her stroke him. The only problem was, he'd have to have his clown's face on, else she'd never go near him. As these thoughts were hurtling through his mind, he heard mummy calling.

'Poppy. Tea's ready.'

'Bye Charlie, see you later,' shouted Poppy, gathering up her bunch of bluebells.

'Coming Mummy, just saying bye to....', but she didn't finish the sentence as Charlie put his finger over her lips.

'Ssh, a little secret', he whispered. So Poppy didn't tell her Mum, just her best friend Olivia.

A few days later Charlie spied Poppy again, this time she was on the side of the road, nearer to the woods. He helped Poppy pick more bluebells and then said, when they were away from the road, 'I'll sit on this log and you can sit on my knee, then I'll do some magic tricks specially for you.'

He made sweets appear from Poppy's ears, from underneath her dress, and then from his own pockets and ears. He felt excited as Poppy's little fingers explored his body, he could inhale her breath, and marvel at her shining blue eyes. The sensations he was feeling were so overpowering that he wanted more. This experience was so exciting, whereas the fumbling quick thrust he'd had with a girl in a garage couldn't be compared. He was so inebriated with his desires that it was only at the last minute that he heard shouting, frantic shouting.

'Poppy, Poppy, where are you?' Pushing Poppy off his knee, he said, 'Got to rush, going to see the dentist.'

'Why, have you got toothache Charlie?' asked Poppy, who didn't like going to the dentist's at all.

But Charlie was rushing through the woods. He'd slipped off his cumbersome boots, underneath which he wore his trainers and was leaping like a mountain goat over branches until he'd left the wood and had reached some disused workrooms. He changed in these quite regularly. Off came the grease paint and the clown gear. On went jeans and a shabby anorak. The folks where he lodged had no idea that this scruffy individual had a double persona. Oh yes. Charlie was cunning. 'Sly as a bloody fox, is our Charlie,' his Dad would announce proudly to his drinking mates. But Charlie was worried. Very worried. He wondered what Poppy would say about the happenings in the wood. But then almost in the same instance, with feral-like intuition he comforted himself with the pictures of Poppy laughing and giggling when he'd tickled her.

'She enjoyed it almost as much as me,' he muttered to himself. Her stuck-up parents wouldn't want to be told that they were in the wrong and should have kept their eye on her. Oh no, so Charlie began to feel more confident that he'd got away with it. Probably not be booked again, he realised, but there were other places.

Charlie stayed in his dreary room for a week or two and then left his lair. Silently he stalked the woodlands. Around the tumble-down shed. Circling his quarry. Alert to the slightest creak. He'd returned for the grease-paint, gaudy clothes and boots. Bundling them into a suitcase he made for the station. Charlie was off to the seaside.

The Chandelier's Story

Enjoyed a very busy day, never thought I would see film crews at Chatsworth. I think Keira Knightley is really attractive and plays the part of Georgiana so well, and Ralph Fiennes is excellent as the non-smiling Duke. I can make these comments with some authority as I was present at all the happenings between that ill-matched pair.

You may already have noticed me, after all who could ignore playful cupids, coronets and scrolled candle holders, all in gleaming silver. Nothing escapes my attention, not the raised eyebrow, not the false smile not the whispers. I'm not only able to see everything, but also to hear everything. I am in on all the secrets, the gossip, the plans, and I have a very good memory. I can tell you a few stories. When I saw Keira Knightley drifting about with those iridescent peacock feathers, an image of Georgiana leapt into my mind, because I can remember when that lady caused a stir, with her incredible wig and tall feathers. If they had got much higher they'd have been giving me a dust. Gambling soirees, extravagant bets, dining and wining, I witnessed it all. Perhaps I could compare myself to Zeus in his kingdom, overlooking the imperfections of man.

When Georgiana was in charge. I say in charge, she wasn't really, and yet she had so many qualities, beautiful, stylish, interesting, but not happy. She and the Duke, the fifth Duke, was not a cheerful character. They would sit at opposite ends of a long table never speaking a word. The silence broken when he called his dogs to fetch tit-bits.

Because they rarely spoke I gleaned my information from the chatter of the maids, as they scoured, polished, and dusted, until the glass and silver fruit bowls sparkled nearly as much as me. Oh, if you're wondering, I'm the oldest of the chandeliers, probably been here since 1694. I knew Georgiana would be expected to produce an heir, but it didn't seem to be happening. I don't think there was much soft talk, the only time I saw the Duke anything like animated, was when he'd got his Whig friends around him.

She was only 17 when she'd left Althorpe, to live at Chatsworth. Poor girl, I felt sorry for her, and I realised that if he didn't show her some proper attention, she'd find it elsewhere. If he had chatted with her he would have found out that she was interesting and imaginative. I overheard some of the Whigs saying that she had written a novel called, 'The Sylph' and that it was quite above the ordinary.

The Duke wouldn't be interested in that, as I said, he only became alive when he held parties for his politician friends, and it was at these occasions that Georgiana came into her own. Could she gamble? Was in debt most of her life and that's another story.

The years rambled on with whispers of affairs, but the Duke, wasn't he a dark horse? Met Lady Elizabeth Foster in Bath, called her Bess, takes up with her and before my eyes we've got a ménage a trois. Trust the French to have a word for it. But I did hear that G., I'll call her that for short, had an affair with a toff called Charles Grey, and there was a child, who was brought up by the Grey family.

So the years go by and everything passes as it always does, but I felt really sorry for G. To tell the truth I've always had a soft spot for her. I reckon her greatest solace was playing the harpsichord, I think it was bought especially for her. But I could tell her health was failing. I have to admit I was glad when I heard that Bess was sympathetic, especially when the Duchess was bled and had leeches applied to her eyeball. Yes her eyeball! It makes you squirm doesn't it? I heard the doctor say she'd got an ulcer in her eye, and I constantly heard her saying that she'd got a headache.

Now when her gambling friends were alone they could hardly wait to whisper about her changed appearance, coarse skin, one eye gone, her neck immense, and she only 40. Only 47when she died. You can't help but feel that she could have been happier if the Duke had loved and encouraged her. But that's life I've seen it happen again and again. And everything passes.

Of course through the years different Dukes have changed this and that, moved the tulip vases and silver candelabras here and there.

Some haven't been interested in the gardens at all, but I think a gem like Chatsworth should have a beautiful setting. Sometimes I imagine how the gardens might be now. I can picture long gravel walks bordered by lobelias, geraniums and perfumed roses, always with a background of rippling water tumbling down from the ancient cascade house.

Through the years we've had a couple of the best gardeners of all time. The first one was Capability Brown, who even changed the course of the river Derwent and harmonised, yes that's the word, harmonised the House with the park and with Derbyshire's hills and woodlands. One flowing into another, quite poetic.

Of course Joseph Paxton was a real favourite of the sixth Duke. The conversations I overheard between them two, Joseph was obviously a friend, he came and went as he pleased. I heard the duke congratulate him when he'd built a high stone rockery with a waterfall and pond. One conversation I shall always remember. The Duke was so excited because Tsar Nicholas of Russia was to visit the next year. I guess the Duke wanted to impress, because he told Paxton that he wanted him to create the highest fountain in the world. You might have imagined that Paxton would have come up with a lot of problems. But no. Within eight months Chatsworth had the Emperor Fountain. Sadly the Tsar never saw it, but through the years, many, many visitors have admired the magnificence of that fountain. It was worth it. Although the Tsar didn't come we had two visits from Victoria, once with her mother the Duchess of Kent and then when she was Queen with Prince Albert. They were treated to a fantastic display of coloured fountains. Fantastic is a new word for me. The sixth Duke was one for making an impression, especially when he entertained royalty, and you can't get much higher than the reigning monarch.

Today Chatsworth and its surroundings are open to everyone to enjoy. For the past few years, we've had hordes of visitors. I couldn't begin to tell you how many file through these rooms. Some do glance up and see me, saying,

'I wonder how much that's worth?'

'How much do you think it weighs?'

'I wouldn't like the job of cleaning it.'

Of course they come from all over, I should think I've heard every language in the world. The locals come again and again.

Christmas time is always popular. We have the tallest Christmas trees, I sometimes wonder how they get them through the doors. For the past few years we've had a theme. I say we, after all I consider myself part of the Chatsworth family. Anyway the theme this year was, 'The Lion, the Witch and the Wardrobe.' Everybody was talking about the wintry, glistening wonderland and the White Witch, whose icy face made you shiver.

Anyway where was I? Sometimes I get carried away. Oh yes, the war years come to mind. There weren't many changes made to the House or the Gardens. We had a college of girls here, that certainly was different. And there were some tragedies and we didn't escape the bombs. Billy Cavendish, was married to Kathleen Kennedy, and tragically killed in action in 1944. Kathleen was one of the famous Kennedy family from America. They are both buried at Edensor.

So Andrew became the 11th Duke and he made the House and gardens really welcoming for visitors and ramblers alike. Deborah his wife, one of the Mitford sisters, was a very keen gardener. Lawns were re-set, hedges designed. One had a strange name called a Serpentine hedge because it weaves in and out like a long green serpent. The Maze is a real winner .The Duchess even won a prize at Chelsea flower show in 1988 with, 'The Cottage Garden'. I had a chuckle to myself when I heard that privet bushes were shaped to resemble furniture.

Andrew and Deborah were a real team. I've heard so many compliments about them. I can tell you they were really popular. When the Duke died in 2004 we were all very sad. The Dowager Duchess lives in Edensor and now Peregrine and Amanda, the twelfth Duke and Duchess have taken over, and everything is flourishing, which brings me back to where my story began, with film crews and film stars. Chatsworth now a rising star of the big screen, Mr. Darcy's home in 'Pride and Prejudice', and historically perfect for 'The Duchess'.

The day's drawing to a close. Evening is here. Film crews have left. Visitors have left. Silence. Doors locked. Alarms set. In the shadowy room I sparkle in the darkness, like a diamond on black velvet.

Chatsworth rests.... but is prepared for whatever ....

Losing Face

'Just off love,' Adrian shouted, as he left the house to attend the Good Neighbours Watch committee meeting. Pam's reply went unanswered.

'I spend so many evenings on my own I'll soon be able to have a complete conversation with the cat,' she muttered, whilst stirring the gravy. I wish my husband wasn't such a wonderful do-gooder. But I might be worse off. She was thinking of Sandra, her best friend whose husband had just left her. No fear of that with our Adrian, she reasoned. He's got appearances to keep up. Every night the same ritual. Dashes in from work, rushes his meal, that is if he's time to eat at all, and then to scouts, parish council meetings, and the forum. The whole of his spare time devoted to others.

At the neighbourhood watch meeting all the affairs were proceeding as Adrian would have wished. Of course he was in the chair and the rest of the committee usually let him have his own way. He droned on about being a watchful neighbour and then quite suddenly declared the meeting closed. Bob, who had nearly been asleep returned to consciousness just as he heard Adrian saying, 'I close the meeting at 7. 45pm.'

At 10pm Adrian tiptoed up the stairs, hoping that Pam would be asleep. But no, she was reading "The Web of Desire".

'I should take your bed to the next meeting, you get later and later. Whatever do you talk about for three hours?'

'Oh its some of those old chaps, like Bob, that always ramble on.' However he realised that Pam was caught in the Web, and he needn't explain his lateness any further.

The next day on her daily visit to Tesco, Pam met Bob's wife, Thelma, and after a few pleasantries said, 'These parish council meetings go on a bit don't they? I said to Adrian last night, Why don't you take your bed?'

Thelma looked at her oddly, and said, 'I wouldn't say an hour's overdoing it, I wish they were a bit longer. He's back before Corrie's finished and I keep missing the ending. Hey, are you OK? You've gone ever so red, you look as though you need some air. Are you on the change?'

'May be, anyway I'll have to dash.'

'But you haven't done your shopping,' shouted Thelma at the fast disappearing figure of Pam.

Immediately at Sandra's, Pam dived into the subject of that snake Adrian. With Sandra, she had a comrade in arms for her friend hated every man who had ever breathed. After two or three schooners of gin topped up with a spot of tonic, a plan was hatched. Pam was to become a stalker.

She slid behind the tree. It was a pleasant evening, and the air was sweet. But she was on a mission. Positioning herself, so that she was able to see the forum committee members. Their faces were turned towards Adrian, and he seemed to be jumping up and down, as if he was on a pogo stick, not in charge at all. Pam was enjoying the spectacle, because Adrian was always the leader, the controller, the pillar of society. She was becoming so interested that she was shocked when she saw Adrian get his coat and dash towards the door, leap down the steps of the village hall and race down the street.

'Oh dear he'll be home before me,' Pam muttered, 'now I'll have to say I've been to Tesco to get some butter.'

Contrition was consuming her. How could she possibly have thought that her wonderful husband had strayed? But when she entered the house, to her amazement, he was marching around the settee, shouting and uttering every swear word known to man.

'What's the matter my darling?' Pam was full of regret and had decided that she was going to be so affectionate.

Adrian yelled, 'What's wrong? What's wrong? I've been accused of fiddling the Forum's funds.'

'You?' Pam uttered in amazement, 'Well, they've got that wrong, very wrong, and they better be ready with a big apology. Everyone says you're the pillar of the community.'

Adrian sank into the settee and began to stutter.

'Come and sit with me, I just want to explain something. You see I did have to borrow £300 a few weeks ago.'

'£300, whatever for?' gasped Pam, and then suddenly like a thunderbolt, Pam's intuition snapped into place. The late nights. The mystery was solved. The explanation was obvious.

'You've got another woman, a bit on the side. That's where the £300's gone. But who is she? Who .... is .... she?'

Adrian was amazed at Pam, a vicious threatening woman was facing him with a red face and piercing, unblinking eyes. Was this his demure little wife?

'You won't know her,' he mumbled and she came onto me, and I was going to finish it tonight.'

'Who is she?' Pam screamed.

'Mrs Royston,' Adrian whispered.

'Oh that's interesting. You mean that permanently tanned woman, who shops in Tesco, wearing just a thong under the tightest white shorts, and who wears sparkly tee shirts that are two sizes too small. Oh Adrian, whatever did you see in her?'

With that rhetorical question hanging in the air Pam was galvanised into action. Jumping up she raced upstairs. Gathered a few clothes. Pushed them into a battered suitcase. Hurled it downwards. She followed. Rammed the case into Adrian's chest, who seemed to be mesmerised by her speed.

'Now get round to your tight little-arsed friend and see if she'll lend you £300.'

As she was uttering these words she was pushing Adrian backwards towards the door. As he arrived in the cold night air more abuse was being hurled at him.

'By the way I've changed a word in that sentence, "Pillar of society". I think it should be "pillock". Yes, it has a better ring to it. "Pillock of society".'

Jack and Jill

Jane Sanderson recently widowed, was pacing around her well-appointed house like a creature, without a place to rest. She had turned on the radio, but the shipping forecast followed by farming information was not what she wanted to hear. The photographs of her and Tom had been put away in the little cupboard under the stairs.

'After all,' she muttered, whilst blowing dust off the orange finned fish from Murano, 'who wants to be reminded of cruises and tropical holidays, when they're over, kaput, finished?'

Why was she up so early? Why hadn't she carried out her pampering routine? Why had she eaten three chocolate biscuits? Perhaps Rosie her long-life friend would have some answers.

At 11 o'clock Jane was in her favourite coffee bar, 'The Bella Vista', waiting for Rosie who was always late, and always arrived out of breath and with a plausible excuse.

'Oh, so sorry,' she said, 'couldn't find anywhere to park,' as she gave Jane the huggiest hug, enveloping her in a cloud of Celine Dion perfume. 'How are you? Have you slept? Have you been to the doctor's?'

'Let's order coffee first', said Jane. 'Carlo, an espresso and a latte please.'

As they drank their coffees, Jane felt she was under scrutiny, concerned scrutiny, as Rosie said, 'You're not well are you, and whilst I'm speaking, I realise how hollow those

71

words must sound. I can only imagine that at first you can't believe it's true and anticipate that Tom will be driving down the avenue at half past five. Opening the door as usual, and saying, that smells good.'

'Yes, absolutely right. But now after a year, reality stark, cruel reality has hit me. Tom is never coming back, I will never see him again. He will never again open the door, give me a cuddle, a kiss, or a smile.'

She sensed that Rosie was struggling to find some words, to comfort her. She knew that Rosie would have liked to say, 'Everything will seem better tomorrow,' but sadly losing your soul mate wasn't like having a sore throat or a bad back.

'I've got to grieve,' said Jane, as she wiped her eyes with the paper serviette, and with that spoken acceptance she felt that she was on the road of recovery. Although she pictured difficult times, and a lot of stumbling blocks, there was a glimmer of light. She knew that Rosie felt that too.

The most difficult part of the day was in a morning, when she woke up, alone. Wishing so much for Tom's cuddle. As she lay there her mind chewed over Tom's last days and then moved to happy holidays and good memories. 'At least I have those,' she would say to the bedroom walls. She had strange feelings that Tom was buried deep within her psyche, like a gritty stone, needing to be polished and smoothed, like a diamond, so that she could carry him with her, and yet could function. But now with dogged determination and forcing herself to do it she was beginning to take an interest in how she looked. What she ate, and not feeling too guilty if she laughed.

'It's time you googled one of those dating sites,' stated Rosie as she spooned the froth from her cappuccino. 'They say "Jack meets Jill" is a good one.'

'I'm not sure,' said Jane, as she popped a sweetener into her coffee, 'It is two years since Tom died, and I do feel lonely; not so much at night when I can sip a G and T, but in a morning when I've to face the day.'

When they reached the car park, Rosie took her friends arm, and whispered, 'Every Jack needs a Jill. Go for it girl.'

A few weeks later she was in the car park of the Swallow hotel. It was spacious. Thank goodness, Jane thought, because I might still have managed to drive into the rose-beds or onto the clipped lawns. Her heart was thumping and her black patent high-heeled shoes felt like hiking boots, caked in mud. Was she insane? Rosie would never forgive her if she chickened out. Her friend would be waiting for a detailed report of the meeting with Mr. Jonathon Edwards. After all she confided to herself, it's only lunch. But how could she be meeting another man? Tom was, is the love of my life. The desire to rush back to the car was overwhelming, but then a little voice in her head repeated, 'It's only lunch, get it into perspective.'

She entered the reception area, which was decorated in grey and white, quite minimalistic. Her image in the mirrored wall, confirmed that she was appropriately dressed. The black and white spotted dress, was a winner, smart but not over stated. Gripping her black handbag she steeled herself and strode purposefully towards the restaurant, her eyes scanning the interior for a tall fair haired man in a light blue shirt.

There he was sitting at a table by the window. He was almost like the description, although perhaps older than his photograph had shown. Forty-five? He looked closer to fifty-five. Was she mad? She wanted to run back home, but her legs propelled her forward and her lips moved into a smiling position.

At the table Jane was ready to chat. He seemed very courteous and had very white teeth.

'Jonathon Edwards, pleased to meet you Jane.'

'Pleased to meet you too, lovely hotel, I've never eaten here before,' said Jane, as she gratefully sank down onto her chair, feeling that her legs might give way at any moment.

During the goat's cheese starter, Jonathon said, 'Better give you a few details about myself. Always been in finance, big finance,' whilst he was saying this he winked at Jane. She didn't know whether to interpret the wink as meaning shady dealings or world-shattering banking negotiations.

Jane hoped she was conjuring up the correct expression on her face, as Johnny, his preferred name, was describing, his numerous hobbies, mingled with mouthfuls of sea bass.' Always kept myself in good shape, with various sports, golf, tennis, sailing, you name it, I've done it, and although I say it myself, very good at them all. Have you any hobbies?.... Sorry, forgotten your name.'

'Oh, don't worry about my name,' said Jane, 'much more interesting to hear about your sporting prowess. Please tell me more.'

Johnny did. Jane realised that he really liked himself and she didn't like him at all. Certain words flowed through her head as she consumed her delicious crème brulée. Arrogant. Self-opinionated. Boring. She'd probably be able to think of a few more before she met Rosie tomorrow. The meal came to an end. He offered a liqueur, but as Jane was driving she had a valid excuse.

'No thank you I'm driving, and I'll have to dash. Got to meet the children from school.'

'The children!' he stuttered.

'Yes, I didn't have chance to tell you, I've got three, all adolescents. Difficult time for parents. Enjoyed the food. Thank you Johnny.'

In her driving mirror, she saw a dejected man, and guessed that three teenage children, would put anyone off. How did she think of it?

Next morning in the Bella Vista, she was awaiting the arrival of Rosie, who came through the door like a kestrel about to hone in on its prey. While still out of breath she managed to gasp, 'How did it go? What was he like? Was he dishy? What car did he drive? Was he divorced?'

'Sit down. Take your coat off. I will confess all to my Mother Superior,' Jane said, as she sipped her coffee that had miraculously arrived.

'Seriously now. I was so taken with him. We ate. Ordered a room for two hours. Made mad passionate love.'

Rosie burst out laughing, picturing the scene, her friend, having it off, with a stranger.

'Seriously,' she said, whilst wiping up coffee froth that had ebbed onto the glass table, 'tell me really how it went.'

'It didn't,' said Jane.' He talked incessantly about himself. How wonderful he was at everything. How he'd been everywhere, and how he'd got exciting plans for us. Oh, the meal was excellent. We'll have to go to the Swallow, some time.'

'You didn't like him?'

'You've got it. I even told him I was the mother of three teenagers. That really halted his plans for us.'

'There's plenty more fish in the sea,' Rosie said, 'remember for every Jack there is a Jill.'

'Rosie, listen to me this event has done me good.'

'Has it really?' said Rosie, smiling as if she'd won the lottery.

'Yes it's clarified some thoughts that have been torturing me. I don't need or wish to have another man, at the moment. I still love Tom.'

'Are you sure? Won't you be lonely?'

'I'm going to join a painting class, I've always wanted to have a go at water colours, and I'm going to volunteer to work a day in the hospice shop. They're always wanting volunteers. And I enjoy my outings and lunches with you.'

Rosie squeezed Jane's hand and said,

'I do too.'

'I don't want to depend on someone else for my happiness. Yesterday showed me that I'm not ready for another commitment. I can choose, and at this moment, I choose to go forward alone.'

The Letter

The letter has arrived, it is hiding between a catalogue advertising exotic holidays and my writers' magazine. I notice that the handwriting is neat, and controlled. I can see the Truro post mark. I could imagine that style of looped letters on a slate chalk-board. I very much want to open it because I think it will complete the jig-saw of my great-aunt Annie's life. But before opening it and I really have to exert self-control, I must explain the events, leading up to this moment.

Grandma previously had never spoken of great-aunt Annie although, she would reminisce for hours about all her brothers and sisters. One afternoon, whilst I was handing grandma yet another cup of tea, she suddenly announced that she had had a sister called Annie.

'She'd be my great-aunt then?' I said, pulling a chair up close to hers, 'you've never mentioned her before.'

'No,' Gran said, squaring her shoulders, 'and I'll probably never mention her again. So Patricia Hodkin you needn't start with your questions. I'm not on Mastermind.'

'Oh Gran, sounds mysterious. Tell me more.'

Totally ignoring my request, she said, 'I'll have a couple of digestives with my tea. And will you put on 'Pointless', I like that programme and I like that Alexander.... something, who runs it, my kind of man.'

I knew for certain the subject of Annie was well and truly closed. But not for me. It took a little research and a few questions to other members of the family, which, by the way, were answered guardedly. But sufficiently detailed for me to be on a train heading south.

I am here in Truro standing outside this imposing building. A solid wooden door faces me and I am hoping that when the door opens, my words will flow coherently. I've practised them a few times, once again I repeat to myself.

'I believe this is the Convent of the Epiphany and that my great-aunt was a professed sister here for forty-nine years. I'm Patricia Hodkin and am doing some family history research.'

Opening the door is a lady of slim build with hair the colour of a glossy chestnut, shaped to frame her pale, unlined face. I am always conscious about colour, and notice that she too has an artistic eye. Her marigold silky blouse complimenting her complexion and coppery tones perfectly. She shows no surprise at a stranger appearing at the door, perhaps the convent has many visitors. She introduces herself as Mrs Wilson. I deliver my well rehearsed introduction and am invited into the hall. An aroma of lavender scented polish surrounds me, and immediately my attention is directed to an ebony board above my head. In gold scripted letters, it's there. Sister Annie S.O.C.E. 1890-1988.

'That's my great-aunt,' I say proudly, 'I think she became a novice nun in 1939.'

'Would you like to have a look round?' Mrs Wilson asks, taking my arm and guiding me towards a curved staircase. I can imagine black robed nuns passing quietly up and down acknowledging each other with a nod and a smile. I feel like Ali Baba in the fairy story, finding the treasures of the cave. Now perhaps I hope I will be able to fill in the last piece of the jig-saw puzzle and find out why Gran refused to talk about her sister. I'm here climbing up the same staircase, holding the same moulded handrail as my great-aunt had done.

We visit the chapel with its large carved cross that Mrs Wilson says has come from Oberammergau and the dining-room, and bedrooms. It is these narrow rooms that make the deepest impression on me. White-washed walls, providing a stark back-cloth to a jet-black cross, its blackness relieved by a silver star. I imagine the nuns spending time in their rooms praying, meditating, quite alone with their thoughts and possibly very weary after a day's hard work. There would be no distractions here. No perfume bottles, or chrome branches draped with necklaces, or cascades of scarves covering most of the bedroom door. I'm thinking of my own bedroom. Cluttered!

I am feeling puzzled as I haven't seen any nuns, or heard any sounds, I'm curious.

'Mrs Wilson,' I asked hopefully,' are there still nuns living here?'

We pause to admire the view of sloping lawns and circular beds of shrubs parading every leaf shade from acid-lime to holly green.

'No not anymore, the last two nuns, left last year, Sister Caroline and Sister Rosemary. It is now a defunct order. And this is to become a home for retired Church of England Clergy. I'm acting as caretaker-cum-receptionist. I was a secretary here.'

I'm feeling downhearted. I had been hoping to talk to a nun, who might have known my great-aunt.

I realise that my tour is coming to an end, as we are back in the hall.

'Mrs Wilson, are the two nuns who left last year still alive and would either of them have known Sister Annie?'

'Sister Rosemary is and lives near, she's very elderly, but quite astute. She may very well have known your great-aunt.'

'Would it be all right. Do you think?' I say hesitantly, 'to give me her address, so that I can write to her?' 'I've been researching Annie's life and to learn about her from a nun, who was here with her, would be wonderful.'

'I know Sister Rosemary and I'm sure that would be all right.'

Mrs Wilson shakes my hand and I step onto the gravel path and into sunshine. I feel like skipping as Julie Andrews did in the Sound of Music. To think I would be able to complete my research. I am looking forward to travelling back to Yorkshire to write to Sister Rosemary.

Before I leave I decide to absorb the building. Take it all in. My overall impression is one of greyness. The walls have a granite look. A bay of arched windows is an interesting feature and high up in the leaden roof are two attic windows, but the most attractive feature is a cupola. It reminds me of a dovecot, white with a roof of copper. To imagine great-aunt Annie living here, working here and it would have been hard work. I'd wheedled out of great-uncle Harry that she'd had no money and so was a sister of the second order, who'd entered the convent without a dowry. But I assure myself there would have been fun and a satisfying sense of purpose.

The following day I catch the train home. I feel puzzled, everything I've learned from Mrs Wilson about the Sisters of Mercy is admirable. Surely grandma would not be so mysterious and stubborn about her sister Annie becoming a nun, and leading such a selfless life. A life to be admired not shunned.

I leave Truro's cobbled streets and its majestic cathedral. A long journey lies ahead of me it will be some hours before I see York Minster. From the window I spy fields rivers and rows of houses with well kept gardens and I even can see a post man emptying one of Her Majesty's letter boxes. The train halts at Bristol, Cheltenham, Birmingham, Derby. All the stations looking very similar as people hurry to and fro with a variety of coloured cases, bright pink, aluminium, striped and spotted. Students with massive canvas holdalls and the practised traveller with just a haversack. On the train goes to Sheffield and finally I arrive in York. Out of the station, to be greeted by the stalwart City Walls, edged all around by banks of trumpeted daffodils, an incomparable golden fanfare! Now for home, slippers and a cup of tea. Tomorrow the letter.

By lunch time my letter to Sister Rosemary is completed and ready for posting. I'm eager for her to receive it as soon as possible so I buy a first class stamp and slip it into the box outside the city's main office.

And now, the reply is here. I discard the holiday brochure and put aside my magazine. This deserves my full attention. Excitedly I slip the letter out of its envelope. Will I learn why her name had never been mentioned, and why grandma was so adamant about closing the conversation?

My dear Patricia,

What a wonderful surprise to have received your letter. I recall your great-aunt speaking of you very fondly. She was like a mother to me. We spent many happy hours together, producing Nativity plays and making lots of angel costumes. The children loved her and she would see how many could hide under her cape. We set up a Sunday School at Malpas, in a beautiful spot by the river, and although we had to walk six miles there and back Annie never complained. You asked me if she'd ever told me of any unfortunate happenings in her life.

The only sad happening she mentioned and which I think estranged her from the family, was this one. Just once she mentioned it. Self-pity wasn't for her.

One Sunday whilst we were walking, I recall her telling me about her love for a rector, who she had really hoped to marry and was convinced that he had the same feelings for

81

her. She had told the family and the girls at the mill of her expectations. She said that in the village she'd become the main topic of conversation.

One Sunday, with a full congregation her hero, the love of her life announced that he had some wonderful news. She said her heart started beating fast and her sisters were nudging her and her brothers winking. Then.... standing by him in front of a beautiful flower arrangement of white lilies and greenery, that she had done, was Olive Knighton! Her friend! She said she had never felt so desperate, so stupid, so humiliated, her legs so weak that she had to sit down. Enveloping her was the shame and anger of her brothers and sisters.

After that she had a miserable time at home and at the mill..She couldn't understand how she'd got it so wrong. The rector had always been asking for her help with the Sunday School, and the bazaars and the flower arrangements and she had mistakenly presumed that he loved her. After months of feeling down she knew she had to save herself. She felt that she was drowning in self-pity and the rest of the family said that, she'd humiliated them and hardly spoke to her.

Eventually with some determination she described how she'd scrambled through the darkness of rejection, prayed a lot and the solution came to her. She would devote her life to God as she knew that she felt content when caring for people, and at peace when attending Church. Very soon after this realisation, she took the first steps towards a new life and travelled to the convent to become a Postulant. From that moment she knew she had made the right decision and was fulfilled and happy.

In our spare time she would play a small harp and we would have a sing-song. Of course we also had our chores, washing, starching and ironing all the Ecclesiastical robes of the clergy from Truro cathedral and of the other churches in the parish. We also worked in a nearby convalescent home, preparing meals and chatting with the patients.

She made some good friends and enjoyed going on holiday with them and would always return with lots of humorous stories. She was a great raconteur. One of her friends would send her a gift of 'After Eight Mints' at Christmas time. The parcel would arrive in a rather battered fashion, the mints all squashed, so I would make sandwiches of them and when we had guests they would say, "We've never had these before!"I wish I could have spoken with you and given you a hug, but writing this letter has stirred many happy memories of my dearest friend Sister Annie.

God's rich blessings,

Sister Rosemary S.O.C.E.

I read the letter again, absorbing every word. My emotions are like the swinging giant pirate boat at Alton Towers. I feel Annie's distress, humiliation and loneliness. I could imagine sleepless nights and tormented days. An outcast in a family where emotions were hidden and where the maxim would have been, "hard luck get on with it". Rejected on all sides, and rejection is very hard to bear. The family's view was that she'd made fools of them, their pride was hurt and she was not going to be forgiven But surely now with maturity and the passing of time, their attitudes must have changed. No one of the family would know that she'd played a harp, I imagine that they would have realised how hard she would have had to work. I guess she would have the same maxim as grandma, "Hard work never killed no one".

I wonder and suspect that grandma had mentioned Annie deliberately. I wouldn't be surprised, because she knew I was interested in our family history and would delve deeper.

Perhaps.... yes.... maybe, tomorrow whilst dipping Digestives into her cup of tea grandma will be my unsuspecting audience, for the reading of the letter.

Sun.... Sand.... and Sacrifice

The kick was accurate it penetrated deep into Samir's ribcage and rendered him breathless.

'Get your bottles and sand.'

His father's voice was like the growl of a ravenous dog. Scrambling over the rough tiles Samir grabbed a piece of bread, a bottle of water and an orange. This would have to suffice him for the day. And like every other day his head would throb and his back would ache as he sat at his rickety wooden table, filling the glass bottles with coloured sands.

Samir ran through the village, his flip-flops acting like scoops, collecting pebbles and grit that grated between his toes. The precious glass bottles, that he'd collected from the rubbish dump, chinked in his satchel. 'Better not break any,' he muttered as he hurried along between the rows of low, white buildings that housed Jordanians, who found life unrewarding and harsh. Soon he was entering the gulley, the hidden entrance to the ancient city of Petra. Its sides were steep and craggy, forbidding the rays of the sun to enter. This was a shadowy cool place, and where some of the tourists rode on donkeys, an added thrill to pretend they were merchants of long ago.

It was early, the sun was just rising and fingers of sunlight were beginning to creep across the Treasury House illuminating the rose-pink stones of two thousand years ago. He'd gleaned his knowledge about his daily work place by listening again and again to the guides, who holding umbrellas or flags, lead tourists like herds of goats around this place of unrelenting heat. He was unsure how he'd learned the necessary phrases in English, German, French, Spanish and Italian, he'd just absorbed them. He attracted his customers, by shouting 'Good morning, Bonjour, Guten Tag or Buon giorno' and giving them his practised smile that showed gleaming white teeth. Although no one had actually said it, Samir recognised that he was a wonderful salesman. Tourists were attracted to him. They would stand in the prickling heat watching him as if mesmerised, by his quick movements, as he poured coloured sand into discarded Cola and perfume bottles. They gasped and pointed at the bottle as black camels set against a back drop of creamy dunes and cloudy skies appeared, as if by magic. Above this scene a band of lotus flowers would deftly appear in turquoise and brown.

At midday even Samir could retreat into a shaded spot to eat his meagre lunch, and then back to work. Although he'd noticed that there were never as many tourists in the afternoon when the sun was at its most powerful. He was in no doubt that its rays could pierce the flimsy parasols and sun-hats, making pink-skinned travellers even pinker and slower as they ambled round the 'archaeological wonders'. Words that Samir had heard the guides say.

He accepted that his life was work. Work that made his back and neck ache and that as soon as he'd get home he would be sent out again to search for discarded bottles, for the next day's labours. He had just one day's holiday, the feast of Eid El Kebir. Every evening he hoped he would see a sheep tethered to the drainpipe of his house and that would signal a day's holiday.

Baa baa, Samir paused, could he believe his ears? He sped round the corner of the house and there the best sight in the world a sheep. He knelt beside it, enjoying its warmth, a warmth so different from the sun. He revelled in its plumpness. Resting his face against its pulsating flank. Relaxing in its closeness, so comforting and beautiful. He even loved its earthy smell.

'When's Eid mamma?' he asked, hoping that his wonderful sheep would have a few more days to live.

'In six days and don't get too fond of it like last year,' his mother replied, as she baked bread in the earthen-ware oven.

Samir was happy knowing that he would be having a holiday. But the thought of watching the slaughter man's knife slice cleanly through the neck of his newly found friend, was too painful to picture. Yet as at all the other times he would not let his father or brothers see his tears. Every man of the family had to watch and watch until the sheep's blood had drained into the dust, staining it for days.

He'd been glad, when he'd heard the story in the Koran, that Abraham had found a sheep and sacrificed that instead of his son Isaac, but now he wished the sheep could be saved as well. He daren't tell anyone of his thoughts. And now today bleating was everywhere. His father reminded him many times that money was needed to buy a sheep for Eid. His sand-pictures had helped buy that cuddly creature outside, which in a few days would be slaughtered.

Samir was up early, as was every family in his village. The day of Eid had dawned. He could hear the words 'Eid Mabarak' ringing through the dusty streets. Soon he was standing in the family circle. His eyes drawn to the shining knife. It hypnotised him. The glinting steel held him. He stood as if rooted to the earth, as the deft hand holding the enemy sliced through wool and flesh, blood, ruby-red blood gushed in spurts and disappeared, soaking into the barren soil.

His friend, his warm comforting pet was gone.

The fleece was removed swiftly and soaked in salty water. His mother cut a piece of meat and cooked it. Then there was a feast, and Samir enjoyed the change of diet and seeing his father laughing and smiling. But he never quite managed to obliterate the scene he'd just witnessed. Perhaps one day, as year after year passed, he would become immune to the slaughter, like his father and brothers.

Next day Samir was back in Petra, surrounded by tourists fascinated by his small hands grasping handfuls of sand and filtering it through his fingers. Miraculously making layers of pictures that brought gasps, 'Marvellous! How clever! Beautiful!' One tourist a lady from England had visited him regularly and always bought one of his bottles and paid generously. Samir imagined her taking his bottles back to her home, probably a lovely house surrounded by green lawns with roses growing around the doorway. He'd seen some pictures of England in a magazine at the barber's.

He wondered if when she glanced at the bottle that she would remember him?

In the sun, ...making pictures with sand.... not knowing his thoughts were of a sacrifice.

The Golden Wedding Anniversary

Here I am sitting in all my finery. I reckon I could light up any room, even if there were a power cut. Buying all this stuff has taken a lot of effort. Rosa had to come to town with me 'cos I'm not too good on my feet these days and my knee could give way without any warning. Believe you me, there's no joy in getting old. Trouble is you think it'll never 'appen to you. It sort o' creeps up on you. Before you know it you've got a chemist's shop in the bathroom cabinet. Then because your memory's not as good as it was, you can buy plastic boxes for your tablets, boxes that are divided into partitions for the days in the week etc.

But I had my eyes opened when I went to town. I said to Rosa, 'Every young'un passing by has got a tattoo, what's that all about?'

'Oh it's the fashion, some have a rose on the ankle or a butterfly on the shoulder,' she said.

'It were only folks who'd been in prison who had tattoos,' I said.

'Times change you know Evelyn, you have to move with the times,' she said, quite sharply, as she armed me along, over the cobbles as fast as she could. I suppose she wanted to get my shopping spree over and done with. She kept saying she couldn't see the point of it. I thought you better look out my lady else you'll be following the other four, so called carers!

'Anyway,' I said, 'shall we go into Marks? It used to be a reliable shop with good materials.'

'OK,' she said. We looked around but everything was so jammed packed, I thought I'm in a maze, I'd never seen so much stuff and some had a posh name 'Per Una'. There used to be a lass in my class called Una. There were flowers squashed between clothes and food. I said very definitely, 'Get me out of here, now!'

Rosa took me to another shop, she said it was higher class than Marks, it was called Primark. Well to tell you the truth it still seemed crowded, but I thought perhaps they're all like this these days. Anyway I got fixed up. I got a shiny gold handbag, a shiny gold scarf, some dangling ear rings and the biggest ring you ever saw, and I don't think I was over charged. I was going to be as bright as that glitter ball that used to hang in the Odeon ballroom. Nobody was going to say I hadn't tried on my golden wedding anniversary.

So here I am, as I mentioned when we first met, when you first set eyes on me. I'm here in all my finery, dressed up like a dog's dinner, as my Len used to say.

Pity he's not here, but he's probably looking down on me.